Winning Chance

Stories

by Katherine Koller

Enfield & Wizenty
(an imprint of Great Plains Publications)
1173 Wolseley Avenue
Winnipeg, MB R3G 1H1
www.greatplains.mb.ca

Great Plains Publications gratefully acknowledges the financial support provided for its publishing program by the Government of Canada through the Canada Book Fund; the Canada Council for the Arts; the Province of Manitoba through the Book Publishing Tax Credit and the Book Publisher Marketing Assistance Program; and the Manitoba Arts Council.

Design & Typography by Relish New Brand Experience
Printed in Canada by Friesens

Library and Archives Canada Cataloguing in Publication

Title: Winning chance / Katherine Koller.
Names: Koller, Katherine, 1957- author.
Description: Short stories.
Identifiers: Canadiana (print) 20190056126 | Canadiana (print) 20190056142 |
   Canadiana (ebook) 20190056142 | ISBN 9781773370132 (softcover) |
   ISBN 9781773370149 (EPUB) | ISBN 9781773370156 (Kindle)
Classification: LCC PS8571.O693 W56 2019 | DDC C813/.54—dc23

ENVIRONMENTAL BENEFITS STATEMENT

Great Plains Publications saved the following resources by printing the pages of this book on chlorine free paper made with 100% post-consumer waste.

TREES	WATER	ENERGY	SOLID WASTE	GREENHOUSE GASES
2	**180**	**1**	**7**	**950**
FULLY GROWN	GALLONS	MILLION BTUs	POUNDS	POUNDS

Environmental impact estimates were made using the Environmental Paper Network Paper Calculator 40. For more information visit www.papercalculator.org.

Canadä

FSC
www.fsc.org
MIX
Paper from
responsible sources
FSC® C016245

To Lorne

There are so few people given us to love.
—ANNE ENRIGHT, *THE GATHERING*

Contents

Belovèd by the Moon

A flattened baseball cap jutted from the drift of curb grit and unleashed a flutter of pleasure in Brenda, who probed her anorak pocket for a plastic bag. The hat, once black, sported an oil company logo. Her father had worn a similar cap to protect his bald head at the annual Consolidated Parts Supply picnic or when they walked the neighbourhood together. Brenda depended on his red cap in the garden because the side mesh vented the heat, but also because she heard him instructing her to *keep the bean rows straight.* This solid black cap would attract warmth from the sun. This, her sixth hat rescue this spring, could be a guide for someone, somewhere.

Brenda gloved her hand with plastic, tapped the hat on a tree to dislodge winter dirt, and parachuted it into her bag. She presented the hats to the Goodwill, along with anything else she had no use for. The Goodwill staff called her Hat Lady. "You have so much to give," the shaky older one said last time. All of her lovingly laundered hats had found homes, but she longed to know to whom.

Tying the bag loosely, Brenda continued on. She imagined this oil field cap would go to an open-faced young man, unemployed, new to the city, biceps pale above his T-shirt sleeve. Soon, she'd find children's sunhats. This was the worst: children's heads exposed, their tender scalps, eyes, and ears.

Building up her speed again, Brenda almost missed the yellow. In the shade of an angle-parked electric blue motorcycle, on the brownish boulevard grass, a little shoe. A yellow shoe, sweetly sweaty, still moist. The women who lived at this house were all bikers, but Brenda had never noticed a child before. On the stoop, the oldest, the bossy one, stared down the street, hard. She yelled, "Crazy bitch," then slammed the door. Brenda turned to look.

A lurching figure with a huge mottled dog heaved a stroller around the next corner to the right. Brenda set off as fast as she could. The shoe must belong to the blonde child in the stroller whose bare arm, Brenda imagined, had waved. She might intercept the stroller if she veered off at the end of her block.

Brenda charged up her heart muscles by swinging her arms. Her pace paid off. As she turned up the next street, the furious threesome hurtled toward her. Brenda paused. The dog looked fierce—held firmly by its owner, who had purple and black hair, geometric designs inking one whole arm and the neck, wrists banded in braided leather, piercings of lip, eyebrow, nose and chin, ripped clothing, and a posture that said *get outta my way*.

But, the child. Pink and yellow sundress, bobbing hatless head. The matching yellow sneaker was double knotted on her right foot. When Brenda revealed what was in her pocket, the child reached and said, "Shoe."

Her smile made Brenda want to give her the moon. Brenda bent and gave the child her shoe and the child put it in her mouth.

"Wait," said the girl in black.

Brenda stood, unsure if the command was to the dog, which lunged despite the combat boot stomped on its leash, or to the angelic child, or to her. The girl crouched to retie the shoe and cooed at the child like a dove. Brenda decided it was safe to make conversation.

"I'm glad I spotted you. What a little darling."

"Yeah."

Confused if that constituted a thank you and, if so, whether it was for the effort of returning the shoe or extending a compliment or both, Brenda persisted.

"Are you the babysitter?"

"I'm the frigging mom."

That language and worse Brenda had heard at the subway station, and she kept an iPod (from Goodwill) in her purse in case she must endure it for any sum of minutes. Although the iPod provided no music (she had no idea how to work it), the ear buds were comfortable. But Brenda detected hurt behind the young mother's darkened eyes. And that cooing. Was that a teardrop wiped away by the fingerless leather glove? Brenda's own eyes wept regularly, but never in public. Her weekly trip to the stores cancelled out the desire to cry on that day, anyway.

The girl said, "Got kicked out. She needs to eat."

Brenda assumed that meant the child, not the terrifying dog. The carrier basket underneath the stroller was empty. "Would you like a cup of tea and a cookie for your little one?"

"Cookie," the baby said.

"What a smart child."

"Well, she can hear," the girl muttered. She flipped down the stroller sunshade over the child, picked up the leash, and looked directly at Brenda. "Dog needs water."

Brenda knew exactly what Goodwill-destined bowl she'd use.

The girl and the dog and the stroller and Brenda proceeded together. Brenda persevered on the uneven grass boulevard. The girl kept quiet, so Brenda inquired.

"What's her name?"

"Chandrakanta."

"How ... exotic! What does it mean?"

"Belovèd by the moon."

As Brenda's moon-faced father had loved her. She often sat alone in her father's musty Chevrolet in the dank garage. Sometimes for hours.

The girl paused, pivoting the stroller.

"This one, right?"

"How did you know?"

"I seen you before. Dog likes your lawn."

The dog stopped to poop on her lush spring grass. Brenda babied the lawn for her father, who had taken pride in its health. He last crossed it by ambulance gurney. Five years ago, but each time she fertilized or mowed, the memory was still fresh.

Rather than observe the dog do his labourious business, Brenda plucked out a spare bag from her other pocket and handed it to the girl.

"Take it to the garbage at the back, and come in the kitchen door."

"Don't forget his water."

Brenda unlocked the front door. Only when their eyes met did the girl bend to scoop up. She didn't tie the bag, which alarmed Brenda, who would check the garbage can after this impromptu get-together.

Past tea parties with her father and his chess buddies, who had gifted her early motherlessness with a collection of teapots, seeped into her preparations. While her father and his friends played in silence and smoked cigars, she passed the cookie plate, refilled the tea cups, and watched, soon learning the game and becoming an able opponent for her father. He had secured for her the only job she ever held, twenty-one years as receptionist for Consolidated Parts Supply, but without him she could not go back. His chocolatey cigar smoke came spiralling back inside her head as she decided on the sunflower teapot, a recent treasure from Goodwill, as yellow and cheery as the child's shoe. She longed for Danish shortbread biscuits from a tin.

In her compact kitchen, she heard the gate latch bang closed, and a jolt of anticipation jostled her. Next came a stab of hunger. How many years since she stopped for tea mid-morning? Or entertained company after her solitary egg, multigrain cracker, and black coffee at sunrise? Her lilac tree, heavy with buds in the wind, bustled behind the stroller parked under the blossoming crab. The dog bounded about the yard, wetting every shrub. Another dry spring, but the forecast promised rain this evening.

Rain will wash the world with petrichor, her father's voice echoed. Brenda loved the mineral smell of earth after a rain and she cherished her father's word for it.

"I need the can," the girl said. She hurried in, boots on, handed Brenda the child, and marched her way unbidden down the hall to the bathroom.

Brenda touched the child's cherub hair and carried Chandra, as she decided to call her, to the sink and ran warm water. Chandra splashed in delight, soaking the kitchen window, her sundress, and Brenda's shirt.

"It's only water," Brenda said, not wanting to change her shirt and leave her guests alone. She dried the child's hands on her best dishtowel.

Holding Chandra on one hip as the girl did, Brenda dumped the prodigious black cap out of its bag to soak in the warm soapy water and rinsed the gritty bag to dry on the line later. She half-filled a cup of milk, and tried to feed the child. Chandra wanted to hold it herself.

"Yucky." She spat out the milk, but Brenda had the dishtowel at the ready.

Brenda found a plastic tumbler and ran room-temperature water into it. The child's precious lips slurped and slopped. Brenda wondered about the rejected milk. Maybe the mother would drink it in her tea?

"We don't do cow milk. Only soy."

"Is Earl Grey all right?"

"Herbal is better. Cinnamon."

But Brenda only had the one kind. The girl took the tea but made a face as she drank it. Then she held out her cup for a refill. She ate six Dad's oatmeal cookies and the baby ate two. Brenda felt she should add a little more to the table.

"How about a sandwich? Peanut butter and crabapple jelly?"

The girl ate three, which finished off the bread bag. And a Granny Smith apple. Chandra munched on peeled, diced apple softened in the microwave and sucked peanut butter off a big spoon. The girl threw her crusts and apple core to the dog outside. Brenda remembered an old soup bone she'd been saving and offered it.

"What's his name?"

"Licker." He was licking himself now.

Brenda held out the bone, but the dog's warm tongue on her hand made her drop it on her foot. Luckily, she still had her Nikes on, almost brand new, a find.

"And yours?"

"Kali."

Brenda washed her hands, rinsed the dishes, and wondered if that was the girl's given name or if it was a kind of alias. She asked where they were going.

The delicate skin around Kali's left eye swelled and purpled. "Far," Kali said.

Brenda wondered where she'd go, if she could afford it. She surprised herself by sharing dreams of outdoor adventure, climbing a mountain or a canyon, or rafting down a river.

"I like beaches," yawned Kali.

Kali also yawned through Brenda's retelling of a friend's account of Acapulco, the dangers there.

Brenda had things to do. There was the crossword, which she'd normally start right after her walk, and the groceries today and her weekly run to Goodwill. At least she'd managed to wash and hang the black baseball cap in the time they sat around her little half-moon table.

"Do you want to change Chandra?" The baby looked sleepy.

"Chan." Kali pronounced Chan like Shawn. "Have you got a diaper?"

"We'll improvise."

First they bathed the baby in the sink. Kali held her in the water, tenderly soaped off her bottom, then lifted her into the softest towel Brenda could find. Kali dried the chubby creases while Brenda held the squirmy bundle.

Brenda laid the child on the bathroom rug, brought out some sanitary pads from the back of the linen closet, and snipped the long gauzy ends into two strips each.

"What the hell is that?"

"They're old. But they should work. The ends clipped to

a belt you wore around your waist." Brenda was going to add that it was like a garter belt, but Kali was laughing.

"You wore that? Freaking hell."

Brenda coloured a little. She didn't want to divulge that they were left a lifetime ago by her mother, along with soft towels, fine linen, and fabrics.

Brenda fit the pad under Chan and separated the forked strands to tie one end from the top and one from the bottom, at each of the baby's hips. She made a bow instead of a knot.

She asked Kali, "Do you play chess?"

Kali laughed again and cuddled Chan to her breast. Chan fit her head under Kali's neck. Brenda's eyes rested there until Kali felt them and marched outside with Chan.

When Kali pulled the stroller down into a bed and nestled Chan under Brenda's bulky green gardening sweater, Brenda thought she heard "Crazy witch." It could have been "bitch," but maybe Kali was recalling the motorcycle maven—could she be Chan's grandma?

Brenda set to work washing the baby's blanket. Three rinses released crust, grime, and stains. Pinned next to the black cap, the blanket pirouetted on the line, a pastel plaid of yellow, pink, and blue. Kali flopped on the chaise lounge near the stroller and the dog kept vigil, front paws holding down the bone, gnawing. Kali stretched her bony shoulders, sang to Chan, and lay there, out like a light. Same with Chan. And soon, Licker.

Brenda couldn't go out now, so she got busy. Groceries were low, partly because Brenda did not believe in stockpiling, but mostly because she looked forward to her weekly visit to Safeway, an oasis of colour and motion and purpose. Chandra's milk would do for a coffee cake, along with the last apples, a half-used half-lemon, and cinnamon. At Safeway tomorrow, she might splurge on that cinnamon tea Kali mentioned. And Danish shortbread. Brenda cleaned up the kitchen right to the floor and thought ahead.

What if Kali and Chan had to spend the night? Brenda concentrated at the sewing machine, stitching down that possibility. She fixed a tiny rip in the black baseball cap and a massive split in the baby blanket, still a bit damp, and then hung them up again. Then she stashed her sewing supplies to give space for mother and child in the spare bedroom, once her father's. Chan could sleep in the bed with her mother and they'd leave the stroller outside with Licker.

Brenda thawed a chicken in the microwave and put it in the oven. She seldom cooked a whole chicken unless she wanted a batch of soup. But Kali ate no red meat, and a stewing hen was the closest to that description in Brenda's compact fridge freezer. Chicken soup was perfect for the predicted rainy evening, and for a child who had no other clothes than her cotton sleeveless dress. Tomorrow at Goodwill they'd find some cute things and wash them in Perfex for Chan. Brenda added some old potatoes and carrots, her last onion, and a little garlic to the roasting pan. Because she'd neglected lunch for herself, she scraped out the remaining cream cheese and spread it on saltines while she chopped, but forgot her rewarmed tea in the microwave while she hastened to mix up the coffee cake since the oven was hot. Soon it would smell like home, but tomorrow, no egg for breakfast.

Brenda tucked the dry fluffy blanket on top of her gardening sweater over the slumbering child. The air had cooled. She unfolded her Mexican blanket, a gift from her travelling friend, over Kali. Ladled out in heaping portions, clouds floated above.

After the activity of this auspicious day, Brenda also had to lie down. She didn't mean to but, in the breeze of the open window, she fell asleep. She dreamt of her father again. He dropped her off at Safeway, as he used to while he browsed at the library. She pushed her cart to the cashier and then went around the counter and rang up the items by herself, at a discount!

The rain angling down on the window pane woke her. Did she burn the cake? Goodness! She'd intended to pop up when she heard the timer.

She hurried to the kitchen in sock feet and a daze. The oven and timer were off, but the cake, and her trusty eight-by-eight aluminum pan, along with the potatoes and carrots, had vanished. The chicken, hacked apart: the sorry legs and slim breasts, she guessed, deposited in a Ziploc bag, because that drawer protruded; and no chicken bones lay in the garbage, only a saturated sanitary pad. The rest of the crackers, peanut butter, lone banana, and sanitary napkins went for a walk, good, as well as some hand cream, shampoo, and the top two towels in the linen closet. Brenda's favourite tea towel, the one she'd used on Chan's little hands, along with the damp towel she'd used on Chan's bottom, huddled in the laundry hamper. A plastic ginger ale bottle from the recycling box was gone, full of fresh water, she hoped. Also, of course, her gardening sweater, and several plastic bags. The Mexican blanket. The dog bowl, too, and the soup bone—but maybe it was buried somewhere, fertilizing a tree.

Brenda checked the freezer. No chicken wieners or three-quarters-used bag of peas remained. On the wall, a framed snapshot of Brenda in a Klondike hat, left a blank spot. This stung. Why would Kali take it? So she and Chan would make fun of her, the Hat Lady? Brenda chastised herself for thinking so. Maybe they would remember her like an adopted auntie they'd visit again. Or a dupe, easily robbed.

Her key. Still in the pocket of her anorak, thank goodness. She had lost her spare somewhere in her father's car where she had cocooned herself their first night apart.

Brenda could no longer put off checking her purse. Usually it was hidden on the top shelf of the back entry under the heavy Mexican blanket. She'd withdrawn grocery money yesterday because she was on a strict budget and eschewed credit: four twenty-dollar bills, poof. Brenda felt deflated, like the thin Goodwill bag under the window bench. Hardly worth the trip tomorrow. Well, no groceries, either.

The flashlight! Gone from the bench, its dedicated resting place. Her father's trusty flashlight, its genial moon-face, eclipsed. Sturdy like the rook, her father's preferred chess piece. Ever Ready like batteries to last a lifetime. Stolen, never again to shine her way. She flicked on the outside light.

Her garden, still to be planted, gathered up rain. Rhubarb will be up soon, she thought. Seed potatoes can be halved.

That drat cap, left on the ledge to add to the Goodwill bag, where was it? Brenda imagined Kali at the transit shelter. The hat hid her bruised eye gazing at Chan, bundled in the cozy sweater and fresh blanket, yellow shoes tied on tight.

Brenda held her growling stomach with one arm and with the other, the ache augering her heart. She recalled games of chess with her father after a satisfying day puttering outside, stew bubbling on the stove. He had taught her how to make a budget and live simply. But he didn't prepare her for the loneliness. Or predict she'd abandon the job at Consolidated Parts out of sorrow or that no one at the company ever thought she needed a visit.

Brenda sank down onto the bench. Deep inside her, as

if it needed the strong flashlight out of the way first, came the will to apply for another job. *Not Goodwill*, she could hear Father scoff, much farther away now. As far away as the moon. No, not Goodwill. One day, she'd find another flashlight there. But not tomorrow.

She pictured herself at the customer service counter at Safeway, in a smart staff shirt and sensible shoes, helping people, answering questions. Her telephone answering skills could be put to use. Even though they must have their pick of younger women, Safeway hired many waiting for old age security. The store chimed full of life: music and colourful veggies and flowers and customers who came by every week, people she could get to know. Instead of her morning neighbourhood stroll, she could walk to work every day. If she got the job, she would sell her father's car and take a vacation, maybe with a co-worker, someday. She flipped off the outside light.

Brenda washed her hands and slid the skin and sparse chicken meat off the bones. She needed voices like Chan's and even stories and tears like Kali's. In the pantry she found a carton of chicken stock. After turning down the burner, she ventured outside to cut young chives for flavour. The sky had cleared and the moon, still shy behind parting clouds, promised to be full. Brenda flushed and let her tears fall.

Chan, splashing in the sink, drooling on her peanut butter spoon, sleeping in the stroller. Kali had treated Brenda's home like a free-for-all, like Goodwill. Yet Kali acted for the benefit of Chan. Maybe Brenda would see them at Safeway one day. If and if. She would offer Chan a sucker from a basket of treats she kept for children and smile at Kali, who probably wouldn't recognize her.

"You are," she whispered to Chan, to the chives, to herself, and the dark blue sky, "belovèd by the moon."

Memory Mine

There you go again, my old Jim. Whenever you need to get away from the surface, from the skin of life, down you go, into our backyard coal mine. Eight feet down the ladder, nothing like the real mines you worked in for fifty years. I'm glad you've hung up your miner's lamp. When you were sixty or a hundred feet under pushing coal, Starla and I mostly kept busy to avoid loading each other up with worry.

I liked to be with you down here. When I needed extra coal to bank up the stove, I took my time in the cool below, my way of feeling the earth, feeling the good soil from which you were made, the black coal that made our living. I always felt closer to you down here, too, knowing that if I tapped the coal wall, some vibration would travel, maybe, down the Red Deer River Valley to where you worked.

You told me this story, the one you're thinking about right now: the winter day you trudged in the yard from school and your father had already been to the mine to fill his wagon. "Cold spell coming," he said, pointing out the frantic feeding at your mother's bird table. "Better get this to the neighbours early."

On your way, as dusk fell, the blizzard howled up. The horses whinnied and stopped at a man ahead pulling his wife in a handcart partly piled with potatoes. The young woman sweated and strained in the cold loud dark.

You steadied the horses while your father and the man hoisted the woman and their little cart into the wagon and you all carried on toward the yellow light of a coal-oil lamp in the window of a farmhouse you've never been in before. The men supported the woman, hollering and heaving, while you tied the horses out of the wind.

The farm wife pulled the oilcloth off her kitchen table and guided the young woman to a side room. Her bent-over husband shoved coal into the stove to boil water then joined the group around the bare wood like the four ages of man: the wizened host, your middle-aged father, the distraught young husband, and you, the preteen wide-eyed kid. You jumped at the screams but the others stoically waited for the firm but gentle hushing, the breathing, the measured cycle of labour. The men joined their own breathing, in simple unison. No one spoke the whole time it took to prepare and drink scalding tea.

While everyone was on their second mug, the young woman settled in the easy chair by the stove, her baby already suckling. The farm wife poured yet more tea and offered biscuits. Your eyes softened at the coal lamp beacon, the warmth and shelter for the birth, the secure hospitality of the farmhouse, the mother and child, content.

When the storm let up, your father left the farm wife a good measure of coal for free. The young man gathered all the potatoes left in the cart for her, too, hoping they weren't frozen to the core. You also shovelled a portion of coal into his cart in place of the potatoes. The couple and their baby stayed the night. You and your father headed home.

"That's when," you told me, "I decided to become a miner."

Your dad worked you all summer, but took you to the mine for a job the very next fall. The pit boss knew your father from his coal delivery job, a boon in the winter when the farm lay under yard-high wind-polished snow. Your mine clothes blackened but, once the coal dust washed off, your skin remained pale from being under all day. In the wash house, you sang.

You felt lit up at the mine. I think you were on high alert, aware of the dangers. You said, "Took five years before I was capable, and I learned something every day. The mine teaches you. Your rock sense grows. You do good work, because your life and your friends depend on it. If a guy's doing shoddy work, the knocks run up and down the line, and by wash time, everybody knows."

Fifty-one degrees Fahrenheit, summer and winter. Some guys got so used to the fifty-one degrees that a weekend breeze on the surface would make them sick. You carved out rooms and pillars as you went, sculpting the tunnels, working with the water, the gas, the pressure, the seam.

You always said "a coal miner needs his brains more than his muscle." Otherwise, the roof might come down and smash the brains right out of his head. Mostly, you listened. Every sound held meaning. Creaking and cracking, hissing and swishing, footsteps and rock falls. Shots fired, shovels loading, cars rumbling on tracks. The men: singing from the best of them, cussing from them all, praying from none. And always, sharp picks on soft rock, like antennae, testing the tightness of the roof.

But novice diggers with no right to their own place, they rushed and ranted and plowed beside you. They only smelled money, and it was good money, but strikes, slow-downs, shut-downs, gas leaks, and fires put you out of work more often than you'd like. You saw it happen to them, the ones without pit sense. So did I, every week at the hospital.

I never would have met you if you hadn't broken your leg in three places in a cave-in. Noticed you then but sent you home after the casts were set. The next year, a rock fall shattered your collarbone, and I'd sit a while after my shift to help you pass the time. You weren't like the others, bragging about how many cars you loaded a day, or how much you earned. Instead you told me the story of the young woman who gave birth that night, how coal's got the light and warmth of the sun trapped inside. I said, "like stardust inside out." Your eyes clamped upon me then and I knew I'd be yours and you'd be my Jim.

After that, you only wanted to get back to work and never get laid up again. You thought you needed to be on your feet and earning to court me, but I fell for you before we even spoke, when I pulled dark curls out of your face as you slept off the shoulder pain. Ah, you're feeling it now, that old injury. I wish I could rub some mint oil on your shoulder for you, your shoulders, your chest, your back that I miss so much.

I vowed when I married you that you'd never get hurt underground again. And you never did.

You found this three-foot coal seam when you dug our new well and made this little backyard mine so we'd never be for want. I liked the extra coal in canning season and for jamming and pickling. And to offer families in need, like the gal across the alley with her third baby in two and a half years, in that shack her husband never did insulate, and the nights still so cold.

You whistled your way home that fine spring evening, birds raucous with delight, wind teasing the lilac blossoms, clouds in the sky shaped to entertain you. After all, you'd been reborn coming up that shaft, soaping away the grime in the wash house. You didn't know it would be your last day as a miner. You expected a meal, ready for you, and a wife who appreciated more than you could imagine that another blessed evening was about to begin with her husband and daughter.

The trapdoor to our little backyard mine lay open. You dropped your lunch bucket and ran. You beetled down to me, where I was still clutching the coal scuttle. I must have fallen off the ladder and hit my head. I don't remember. My sweet Jim, I'm sure I died right away.

The dust of inside-out stars in our backyard mine is the last air I took. You inhale deep, like you want to breathe all of me in.

"Ah, Ida," you say, "you were with me in all the rooms I mined. You were there, in my head. The words I heard were yours. Why can't I hear you now?"

Oh, my sweet. We don't need words anymore. Just breathe. Breathe and remember. Feel me, feel my presence.

"Dad? Dad, are you in there? I've been looking all over the neighbourhood."

It's our darling girl, now a busy mother herself. Oh, Starla, be gentle.

"Go away and leave me with your mother," you say.

For you, the deep peace when the babe was born in the farmhouse was surpassed when our Starla arrived, rushing out of me and into the light. For me, nothing ever compared.

"Dad, where's the ladder?"

"I busted it up."

Come home safe, Jim. That's what I whispered to you through the rock. Every day.

"I can't leave you down there all night."

"I need to hear her."

I loved the smell of the earth. It smelled like you.

"Dad, you missed supper."

Starla will take care of you, Jim.

"Go home to Henry and the kids. I've got my beer, my hard-boileds, my apple."

"What about a flashlight?"

"I got one."

"Turn it on. I can't hardly see you."

"Don't want to waste the battery."

"I'm leaving the trapdoor open for air, but it might rain."

"Goodnight, Starla."

You hear her car door close, the ignition.

You pull out a box of matches. And three sticks of dynamite. Oh, Jim.

"Now's the time, Ida. Blow this up and no one will ever get hurt in here again. I'm sorry I ever dug it out. I'm sorry. I'm so sorry."

So am I. Starla's kids, a trio of boys seven, eight, and nine, are curious and nimble enough to get into trouble here, ladder or no ladder.

You strike the match.

But there is a light from above, Starla again, peering down with her emergency flashlight. Henry keeps her car equipped. I love Henry for that.

"Dad, why the match?"

He would never hurt you, honey. He would never. You are his Starla. Put out the match and tell her, Jim.

"After marrying your mother, the best moment of my life was the night you were born."

"I called Henry. He and the guys from the fire hall are on their way."

"You look so much like her."

"After we get you out of there, we're going to fill the mine."

"You even sound like her."

 She is me, now, Jim. Listen to her.

"Bring up anything you want to keep. Your miner's lamp?"

The dynamite. Leave it behind, Jim.

 You drop the lit match. It lands in the bucket.

"The last thing she touched," you say, and pick up the coal scuttle, stare at the match burning out.

"What about her pick axe?"

The one you made me, light and short enough for me to handle. The boys would love it for their fossil hunts.

"Got it," you say, and place it gently in the bucket, the oval of it consuming the points of the pick. I wish I could fold myself into it instead, wrap myself around you every night, coat you in stardust.

"Here comes Henry," Starla calls.

"What's he got the siren on for?"

"He likes me to know where he is."

Take me. Take me with you, my dear. Can you hear me?

You run your hands along the coal seam like I did so many dusky afternoons. You touch your hands on your face, your arms, your neck. Feel my fingerprints.

You'll never be hurt underground.

"Dad, do you want a ladder or the harness?"

Hear me?

"I hear you, Ida. I hear you!"

The Exchange

Molly was the only rider on the squirt-sized bus. The driver slowed down and nodded. So this was it.

"Lucky you," she said to the fake leather gym bag. A dollar at the church bazaar, but she got it for half price by shifting her ragged bundle from one arm to the other. Fifty cents, pinched from the Sunday collection basket. The bag, dirty white now. Zipper didn't even work.

Molly hefted it and stepped off the bus. Someone barbequed steak. She recognized the smoky smell from the restaurant. The guy at The Keg said tomorrow at eleven, don't be late, and ditch the bag.

She turned to the bus driver.

"When do you go back the other way?"

"Half hour, across the street."

"I'll be there." Molly checked her watch. Two dollars at the rummage sale, but small enough to lift. She had to be at work on time.

Even though it was August she wore her parka because

it made her look bigger and she needed it at night. Her lips were chapped from the dirty downtown wind.

Riverview Close. All she had to do was cross the street to the odd numbers and follow the curve to 21. The river view must be in their backyards.

She put down the stinking bag to change arms at the stone path. Flowers in a wave on one side, the big yellow heads above hers. The late afternoon sun beamed on them, like lamps. They looked happy. The door, the same yellow.

She hoisted the bag, walking slowly.

But the birds in the sunflowers flew away. The sound they made, like potatoes on the boil. She held the black metal railing to climb the steps. Flipped up the "Baby Napping" sign to ring the doorbell. Balanced the gym bag on her hip like the sack of apples from Shauna at the food bank.

The door had a skinny window beside it, so she saw Shauna before Shauna saw her. Apron on, even. Tossed it off to the chair to answer the door. Dressed up, in a skirt. Shoes, too. Like she's on TV.

"Yes?"

"I seen you at church. You gave me apples."

"Oh? At the food bank. Sorry, I don't remember your name."

"Molly."

"What do you need, Molly?"

"Why do you gotta go to church for anyway?"

"Excuse me?"

"You got a house with flowers tall as me."

"Sunflowers. You like them?"

"A doctor for a husband. Who goes to church with you. And three healthy kids and a job and you look better than your picture."

"My picture?"

"From the magazine. On the bulletin board."

"Oh, at church. I wish they'd take that down."

"I took it. I got it for you. Hold this load?"

"How did you find me? I mean, my address?"

"Phone book."

Eyes on the bag, Shauna started bouncing like she did at church with her own baby. To calm herself. Molly could read fear. Shauna reached in the bag, picked up the broken rattle, shook it for nothing.

"Quiet one. Boy or girl?"

"Girl, same age as yours."

"Really? So ... delicate." Shauna sniffed. "Do you need a diaper? A bottle? Is that why you came?"

"I like your sunflowers."

"They're my favourite colour." Shauna looked at them for a moment. Smiled at them.

It was all Molly needed. She braced the door open with her foot, slid in, pushed Shauna, cradling the bag, outside with her stupid sunflowers and closed the door. Locked it. Molly didn't have a favourite colour. Never did.

Molly watched Shauna grab the porch railing, stumbling, but protecting the bag against her chest with her other arm. She put the bag down under the mailbox, out of the way. Shauna rapped on the window.

"Hey! What are you doing?"

Molly waited for Shauna to stop hitting the glass.

"I'm pretending I'm you, like in the magazine."

Molly looked at herself in the hall mirror. Her eyes, dark as tunnels. Greasy hair tucked inside the coat, greyish pink. Why have a favourite colour when it only gets dirty? She could smell hamburger frying. Heard the TV in another room.

Couches, soft leather, in the front room. Chairs. Rugs on the floor. A fireplace. Pictures. On every wall. A plant, even, here in the front hall.

"Wait!" Shauna lowered her voice. "That's not visualizing. That's...."

"Trading," Molly said. Her voice was scratchy. So thirsty. All the time.

"But my kids! Your baby!"

Molly tied Shauna's apron over her parka. A bit damp. Molly wiped a hand on the wet spot. Dirt came off on the yellow stripes.

"This fits, anyway."

"What do you want?"

Molly saw Shauna on the other side of the window, her hands sweating on it, making prints. It took a while to think of all she wanted, but Molly could only answer Shauna with a question.

"Why do you have all this, and everything I have is in that bag?"

"She's a beautiful baby." But Shauna kept her eyes on Molly.

"Failure. Failure to thrive, that's what they said. And I gotta work."

They heard, "Yabba-dabba-doo!"

"Is that their favourite?"

"If you turn it off, they'll scream."

"I like *The Flintstones*." She'd seen it at the teen drop-in at church. They had free snacks. After her cousin kicked her out for getting knocked up with no job yet, they let her snooze sitting up, no legs on the sofa, because of her belly.

Shauna's eyes got teary. Then turned away, gazing at the sunflowers again.

Molly pulled out the crumpled page with Shauna's picture on it, from *Modern Parent*. Molly could read Shauna's mind by the bit that was underlined: *Whenever I have a problem, I use visualization.*

Shauna closed her eyes.

Molly read on, *I close my eyes and imagine that the problem is solved. I don't worry about how it gets solved. I exchange the problem for a picture of the resolution.*

She had asked the bus driver. Resolution, that means the ending.

Shauna whispered, but Molly could make it out, "I'm in my house."

Molly read slowly, *I look at that picture in my mind and I know...*

Shauna flipped down the "Baby Napping" sign over the doorbell. Molly's was asleep, too, in the bag under the mailbox. Always sleeping.

Shauna held her hands to her head, eyes still shut. On the doorstep, but far away, babbling on. "Then I went out to weed the sunflowers. The kids played house on the steps with my keys. When the baby cried, we took the stroller around to the back. The kids left the keys ... for grandma. They always make me the grandma..."

Molly looked back down at the page, *I know I'll find a way.*

Shauna reached in the mailbox.

The key turned the lock, the door banged Molly's shoulder, and Shauna grabbed a parka sleeve, yanked her out. Molly's hand hit hard against the metal railing.

The door locked again.

Molly dropped the page with Shauna's picture in the mailbox, slammed the lid, and shook out her hurt hand. The kid didn't wake up. Hardly ever opened her eyes. Molly bent down.

She planted a kiss on her stinging thumb, brushed the baby's forehead with it, and ran down the steps. Shauna opened the door.

"Wait."

Molly hurried through the sunflower walk.

Shauna picked up the bag.

"Molly! Your baby!"

Molly stopped. She held up her hand. Then the other one. Both hands light, like branches to the sky. If she could be a tree. Birds would come to her. Even in winter.

Shauna said, "I can't keep her." But she stayed on the porch.

"Until I have sunflowers, too."

"You could go to the church. Or the clinic, the hospital, the children's aid." Shauna's boys looked out the door.

Molly could make a run for it up the stone path, get the bag, push past them and inside that yellow door. But she'd smash the mirror. That would feel good. With the frying pan. The burnt hamburger all over the plants, the window, the floor.

But she had work. The guy at The Keg said.

Molly picked out a few black sunflower seeds and dropped them in her pocket. She'd never grown anything in her life. Find the right place. Where there's sun. And a river, somewhere.

Molly crossed the street. So tired. The driver would probably let her stay on and sleep until the end of his shift. Then kick her out at the terminal. She'll sneak under another bus. The one time she slept in the open, under a tree in the church parking lot waiting for the Food Bank to open, some dude helped himself, hand over her mouth, and here she was.

"Wait!" Shauna shouted. "What's her name?"

Molly checked her watch. The bus was late. She fished out her transfer and waited at the bus stop.

"Molly, tell me her name!"

"You know that, too, Shauna."

Shauna was doing that dance with the bag again. Shoulders hunched, forehead wrinkled up. Her kids clutched her skirt. Noisy in church, but mice now. Like the bag baby.

"Molly?"

"Shauna."

Molly took off the apron. It would keep her parka dry at the sink all day. Hands, warm in the water. She hoped for rubber gloves. Yellow.

As the bus pulled away, Molly looked back. Shauna had her out of the bag, nuzzled against her neck. Then houses, more houses, but no sunflowers. Molly bunched the apron under her own neck. She rocked gently to the tiny ticks of her watch.

The Care & Feeding
of Small Birds

Cloudy looked out at snow falling like dust. He rubbed his eyes. There was a crust on them. And crud on the sidewalks.

Mom liked the walks swept down to the bricks. Last year, Cloudy did it every other day. This winter, didn't go outside. Not even to go bowling.

This morning, only one red sock left in the drawer.

Mom talked in his head. *Always wear matching socks, Cloudy.*

Clinging to the single sock was a ringlet of white hair, held by thin blue elastic.

"Ha, Mom."

He explored the cut edge of hair with his thumb. He used to feel his moustache like this, but she made him shave it off. Mom's lock of hair buzzed with electricity, like an alarm clock, so he buried it in his pocket. He pawed his beard.

Go slow so you don't cut yourself.

He hadn't shaved all winter either, and he still didn't feel like it. To find a shirt, he forked through the pile in front of his closet.

March 11, beamed his clock as he buttoned his shirt, bottom to top. *1:45 p.m.*

He mimicked Mom: "*Me an old lady, and then the gift of you.*"

Today you're thirty-two.

Already, a curl of her hair as a birthday present. He hoped for birthday pie.

Before winter he had loaded casseroles, stews, squares, and cookies into the deep freeze in the basement for Mom.

In case I die.

All winter he brought the frozen food up, one container at a time.

Today, one round dish and one square one sat on the bottom of the freezer. He wiggled the toes in his left socked foot, then the naked right ones, cold on the basement concrete. Bent over the side, his head and chest in the chill, he grinned because Mom, five feet tall in her little white top bun, could never reach the last pie plate on the floor of the deep freeze.

The label read, *Peach, for Prayer.* Mom's specialty. He was Prayer's special helper. Prayer called him *my man.*

He carried the pie up the stairs and set it on the counter. Cloudy wondered if Prayer was eating. He'd never seen her cook.

To share.

He patted his pocket. "I know, Mom."

Prayer's sidewalks, like his own, had been waiting. He got on his boots, his coat, and cap. Cloudy had to see Prayer, to explain about the winter. The bear winter.

Always cover your ears, Cloudy.

He pulled the earflaps down.

Mom called him Cloudy. *You never cried as a baby. Instead, your face clouded up.*

"Ha, you're the one who wanted to cry." But Mom never did, even after Daddy ran away when Cloudy was a baby who never cried.

He took the pie and walked to Prayer's. His bare foot inside the boot wanted to warm up so it went faster than the sock foot until they both stopped at the house next door to Prayer.

The monstrosity, she called it. Bulldozers had wrecked the lawn in years of house renovations. Prayer's lawn had a thin layer of melting snow, but this had none. Flat and green as a football field on TV. Cloudy took off his glove and bent down to touch.

Plastic. Like toy grass.

Prayer's sidewalk needed chipping. Prayer would be upset. Junk mail hung out of her mailbox.

Flapping like a flag to say nobody's home.

The doorbell did not work because he had disconnected it. Prayer didn't like people at the door unless they were invited. She feared for her golden statues and the hangings from Burma. Prayer also had him nail a brass plate over the mail slot on the door so the cold air couldn't get in.

Bad for the bird.

Cloudy was in charge of cleaning the birdcage and changing the feed and water for Prayer's budgerigar. Each time Budge the bird died, Cloudy buried it in a special place in the backyard and Prayer poured two glasses of Glenlivet 25 Year. Their secret.

He put the pie down and picked up all the mail, even the pieces in the flowerbeds under the snow blanket.

Take your time.

Prayer was an old lady. Her friends died a lot, so she drank to the dead regularly. Her glass was full but his was a splash because he had work to do.

After, she said, *Now, Cloudy*, and they'd each have a Scotch mint. She washed the glasses and he dried and put them away because he was taller and could reach the cupboards better. *Never drink alone.*

Every time Budge died, the next day he and Prayer would go to Pet World and buy another Budge. Prayer had old eyes so she paid for driving lessons and the tests so Cloudy could drive her silver Oldsmobile. He passed his learner's permit after three tries (Prayer said one didn't count because he was getting a cold that day) and the in-car test the first time. After Cloudy became her driver, Prayer paid him extra. They went to the liquor store for Glenlivet 25 Year and to Safeway for groceries, to the hardware store and the plant nursery, to the doctor and the dentist and the bank. And to Pet World. Cloudy liked going to the bank and to Pet World the best. Pet World was beside Bear Paw Bowling.

Arms now full of flyers and letters, Cloudy rapped the door with his elbow, so it was muffled, but he did it five times anyway, their signal: *Clou-dy's-here-to-work.*

He looked down at the mail. At home there was a spreading hill under the mail slot. Bills, bills. Bills he did not know what to do with. He would fill a Be Kind to Our Planet grocery bag and take the bag to the bank.

"Ha, the teller will tell me."

Cloudy elbowed the door again. He knew Prayer moved slowly so he waited. He wondered if Prayer had gone on holiday to Victoria again with Buster, her son from Toronto. No answer.

Cloudy stacked the mail on the porch and fished for his keys, fanning them out: car, home, Prayer's garage, and Prayer's house, for emergencies only. Prayer would count the overflowing mail an emergency. He popped the key in the lock and pushed open the door to the smell of overheated dust, same as always.

He took off his boots and made two trips to carry the pie and the mail to the sunny kitchen. His bare foot spread wide on the warm hardwood.

"Hello?" Prayer wasn't home but he could hear her voice. *Junk mail is junk.*

He opened the cupboard under the sink to get a recycling bag and knocked over two empty Glenlivet 25 Year bottles that shouldn't be there. They lay on the floor like two bowling pins after a decent roll.

What do you do with dead soldiers?

He wrapped the bottles inside newspaper flyers in the bottom of the recycling bag. He sorted the junk mail out from a few pieces of real mail. The flyers and advertising cards went on top of the bottles in the bag so neighbours and bottle pickers and Mom couldn't see. But Mom could see now.

Oh, I knew, but I never let on. Prayer's the boss.

"No more secrets." Cloudy patted his pocket happily.

Cloudy saved one newspaper flyer for Budge. If the bottles hadn't been cleared out, then what about the cage?

The birdcage was empty.

Cloudy sighed and slowly fetched the key behind the picture of Prayer's dead husband with a giant ibis bird in one hand and the gun that shot it in the other. Cloudy unlocked the liquor cabinet. Inside were one half and two full Glenlivet 25 Years.

He twirled Mom's tuft of hair between his fingers and then tipped the half bottle so the Scotch barely covered the bottom of the glass. "Never drink alone." He dipped the ends of the curl into the golden liquid and turned them upside down. "Here's to Budge."

This was Budge number eleven. He waited for the warmth after two small sips. Then he felt inside the little crystal bowl beside the toothpicks in the cupboard. No Scotch mints. Only two white leftover particles. Prayer must have toasted a lot without him, and no one to pick up more mints at Safeway. He licked the mint specks off his finger.

Better than nothing.

He always felt a bit low until there was a new Budge. So he hummed the happy birthday tune to himself, made a cup of tea, shined a fork, and went at the pie.

But after the Scotch, the song, the tea, and the whole pie, the heavy sadness crept over him. It had held him down like a sleeping bear all winter. He pushed Mom's curls back in his pocket but he heard her anyway.

Time to get busy, Cloudy.

He washed his fork and tumbler and took the aluminum pie plate and the recycling bag to the alley trash. The walks needed doing out back, too. He breathed in the snowy air. If he could clean up at Prayer's, why not the garbage and mess at home? But how, with no radio on loud at six, no eggs over easy, no matching socks, no shirt hot from the iron, no one turning off the TV at night?

When Cloudy had questions, Prayer always gave the same answer: *Maybe you need a wee wooly nap.*

He lay down on the day bed in Prayer's spare room, under the red tartan mohair blanket.

Cloudy didn't hear the front door. Buster wore a black suit. "Look who's here. Mom's man. With a beard. You look like a grizzly. What's up?"

"I brought in the mail."

"How about a drink? Lost your sock?"

Cloudy bent down and changed his sock to the other foot.

As he followed Buster to the kitchen, Cloudy worried if he'd put away the Glenlivet 25 Year.

Good habits are worth keeping.

Nothing left on the counter but his tumbler, not yet dry. Buster gave that one to him.

The liquor cabinet creaked open again. Cloudy thumbed the fluff of hair in his pocket. He wanted to ask where Prayer was.

"Who died?"

Buster held his glass up to the weakening sun. "To mothers in heaven, mine and yours."

"Here's to Mom," Cloudy answered. It was a painful exhale, a balloon of hurt. He paused. "Here's to Prayer." Her name came out cracked, with edges, and tore his heart.

He closed his eyes. He had never liked the taste. But he did it for Prayer. He hoped Prayer and Mom found each other in heaven. Prayer needed Mom to manage, and Mom needed Prayer for everything. They were like sisters. Prayer was almost an auntie to him. And now he was alone. Buster drank heartily.

"She called you to drive her to the doctor's office. I thought maybe you went wild with the allowance she set up for you. Mother was pleased you took a little holiday."

Cloudy's face burned. He remembered that the phone rang for a while, a few days in a row, before it stopped. Buster went on and on like a phone that wouldn't quit.

"She eventually hired twenty-four-hour help. She even sent somebody over to check on you. No answer at your place."

Cloudy didn't recall anyone knocking on the door, but

then he could have been in the basement. Or in a heap, hibernating under a hill of dirty clothes.

"One of them dented her car. After that, Mother took cabs."

Cloudy knew she'd hate that. He wondered if Buster could hear Prayer, too.

Taxis are for tourists.

And Mom echoing, *That's for sure. Strangers at all hours. No privacy. Goodbye peace and quiet.*

His hand drifted to his pocket to silence her.

"Some of the help stole, too. Remember her smiling gold Buddha? Vamoose. I've done an inventory."

Cloudy's chin dropped to his chest.

"In the last few weeks, Mother slept all the time. She welcomed the drugs."

Buster took another two fingers of Scotch, looking deep into his glass. Cloudy was sure both of them could hear Prayer now.

I don't believe in pain.

Cloudy left the last of his Scotch. He sloshed it around while Buster started up again.

"I had to be here on business. That's why the reception was today. I put a notice in the newspaper. Fourteen people came for lunch, most of them oldsters I didn't know, and a few neighbours I did, and the caregivers, her friends. A good turnout and over by three."

Prayer called people *friends* but Cloudy knew all her real friends were dead. Except him. But he'd been under a rug.

"Today's my birthday," he said, and wondered why, with Buster, he felt like he'd woken up, solid against the heaviness, the heat. His bare foot stroked the floor.

Always take another chance. That was Prayer again.

"Too bad you missed it. We had cake. Very elegant, at the Macdonald Hotel. As Mother would have wished."

But Buster was wrong. She would have wanted it at home, with peach pie and her golden statues and gold-rimmed tea-cups and no drafts and her own good Scotch after. And Scotch mints filling the crystal bowl. Cloudy would have passed them around. The mints were the best part. Buster poured himself another.

"Where have you been, anyway? Caused me a lot of trouble, not having someone I trust around here. What hap-pened to you?"

"Mom died."

"I heard about that. Mother had the reception here. Have you had trouble since then?"

Get it out of your head. Once and for all.

Okay, Mom. Okay, Prayer.

"That day, Prayer was not sick or tired," Cloudy said. "She was in charge. We had tea and sour cherry pie from the freezer because that was Mom's favourite. There was Prayer and me and Sally the Safeway lady, Tom from Pet World, and Avelina the bank teller."

That was five. Five people, but everyone there knew Mom and loved her.

Avelina was Mexican, with a long thick braid, and she was smart. Cloudy didn't want to do banking tomorrow in bare feet.

"I have to wash some socks."

"I have to show the house to an agent." Buster corked the bottle. It was down to one-quarter full.

"I'll go clean off the walks first."

Buster yawned. "I'm catching the red-eye back to Toronto."

Married to his work.

"You need a wee wooly nap."

Buster smiled, put on his glasses, and opened the mail. Cloudy went to the front closet. Prayer's rainbow of coats for every kind of weather was gone. The broom stood alone.

The sun had softened the crust, and Cloudy brushed off the front sidewalk in minutes. The light exercise felt like opening a window. Cloudy's job from the age of fifteen to thirty-one had been the upkeep of Prayer's back garden and front yard. Now they could get carpeted like next door.

I have my standards. But Prayer was gone.

Cloudy went in to wash the glass tumblers. He had forgotten how soapsuds settled him and looked forward to the dirty dishes waiting for him at home. His job now, from thirty-two on.

Honest work makes you honest. Mom again.

Buster wrote out a cheque. Cloudy dried and put away the tumblers, looking out at the yard.

"This is a good house. And the garden, too."

"I hope to make a private sale."

Prayer would approve. *Lawn signs are vulgar.*

Buster added, "Probably sell to a buyer wanting to build."

"When was the last time she went out?"

Buster looked at Cloudy over his reading glasses.

"To the doctor, two months ago. After that, her doctor came here."

Cloudy nodded. People did extra for Prayer. But Cloudy had left her to strangers and taxis and AstroTurf. The hurt in his heart bled all through his chest. He felt drained inside, like the sink. He watched it suck the last of the water.

Buster put the cheque in an envelope.

"Now. Keep the walks clear. I want the house key back; you keep the key to the garage and take the tools in it and the broom. Put the mail in the backdoor milk chute from now on."

Cloudy had fixed the milk chute once. Mom had used it as a hiding place for pies cooling. Hot pain, not on top of him like a heavy fur coat, but inside him, in the empty spaces, filled Cloudy up.

On the envelope Buster wrote his phone number in Toronto and said Cloudy should call in case of emergency. Cloudy shoved the envelope in his pocket under Mom's hair so soft. That morning last fall when she didn't get up, he tried to wake her by touching the wispy curls by her ears.

Cloudy turned back to Buster at the front hall.

"Buster, do you think—?" A warm teardrop fell on Cloudy's bare foot.

Buster looked down at his mother's Persian rug. Another drop fell.

"Mother left you the Oldsmobile."

"Oh, no. I can't drive alone. I wouldn't know where—"

"Then I'll cancel the insurance. When it sells, I'll reimburse you."

"Could I … Buster, what about the birdcage?"

"That's my man. An empty birdcage won't sell the house. Looks like something died in here."

The tears kept coming, one at a time. Cloudy reached with his tongue. The salt tasted good after all that Scotch. He put on his jacket and fumbled the keys to Prayer's house and the Oldsmobile off the ring.

Buster returned with the cage and a bag of Budge's food and bird treats and toys, most of them new from Cloudy's last trip to Pet World with Prayer in the fall. Cloudy hooked the cage with two right fingers and put the keys in Buster's open palm and then gripped the bag in his left hand.

"When did he…?" Cloudy bet he was the reason. No water, no food, no cage cleaning.

"He wouldn't eat. So Budge went with her. In her hand."

Prayer spoiled all her budgies. But this Budge stayed with her at the end. Prayer was not alone. Cloudy took a breath that felt like going up the stairs, then a loud sigh. The crying was over. Cloudy would not be alone, either. He put the cage in his bag-holding hand.

Cloudy laid his free hand flat against the wall, to feel its warmth. Prayer's house.

Bye Cloudy. Be well. Her last words. He never did say bye. The day of Mom's funeral lunch, the leftover piece of cherry pie balanced on his palm, he went out the door and sunk into a bear hole.

Buster pulled one of the full Scotch bottles from under his arm.

"Take it."

Cloudy shook his head. Buster held it up.

"I can't fit them both in my suitcase."

Cloudy's eyes remained fixed on the cage, which he took back into his spare hand. Buster waved the bottle.

"Come on. For your birthday."

"It's for dying."

Buster was quiet then, with his two hands gripping the bottle like a rifle, like his father in the dead great ibis picture. Buster, a boy without his mother, without his father, like Cloudy.

"I know why all the Budges died," said Cloudy.

Buster inspected the label of the Glenlivet 25 Year. He turned away and found his hankie.

Hands full, they didn't shake like they usually did.

The next morning when the bank opened, Cloudy had Buster's cheque and the Be Kind to Our Planet bag full of bills and a shaved face and two clean socks on, first in the lineup for Avelina.

"Where have you been?"

"Prayer's funeral was yesterday."

"I know. I had to work. So, we need to change the name on all your bills from your mom to you, with your legal name, Clarence."

"My Daddy gave me that name." It was on his driver's license.

Avelina called to pay and hook his telephone back up. She was firm.

"Bring your bills every week. If you forget, I'll phone you."

Today was Tuesday but yesterday was his birthday, his lucky day, so they decided on Mondays at 11 after the rush so they could take their time. Avelina showed him her business card with her phone number. It even had her picture on it. Then she copied Buster's number off the envelope to the back of her card.

"Keep that in your wallet. And here's your money until Monday." Avelina offered him a mint from the jar and another one for later. He stashed that one in his pocket, where Mom's curl caught his finger.

"Do you like bowling?"

"I never tried it." Avelina flipped her braid behind her shoulder.

He always waited for the braid. That's how he knew it was time for the next person in line.

"Bye, Avelina."

"See you on Monday, Clarence. Eleven o'clock."

He took the bus to Pet World. As he walked by Bear Paw Bowling, someone came out the door and he heard a strike, then a cheer. The strike sounded like his name, Clarence, straight and clear. He would come back tomorrow with his leftover money. He would bowl with himself.

"Ha, no waiting." But maybe, no fun. Maybe one of the workers would play with him on their break.

Inside Pet World, he breathed deep. Wood shavings and lemons. He loved this smell. He looked at all the budgies from both sides of the row of cages. He talked to them. They chuckled to him.

The manager, Tom, shook his hand and was happy to call him Clarence from now on. He was sorry to hear about Prayer and Budge eleven.

The name Budge was from Prayer's dead husband, so the bird was always male and his nose was blue. Clarence knew how to tell the females because Mom had brought books from the library about budgerigars with lots of pictures and they read them over and over. Clarence picked out two green female budgies. He named one Mom and the other Prayer. Mom was a lighter green than Prayer. These two, Prayer and Mom, had noses the colour of his hands.

Clarence helped Tom catch the birds, inspect them carefully, and box them up. Then he counted out his cash.

"I know why all the Budges died."

"Why?" Tom's eyebrows went up.

Clarence murmured gently to the birds one by one as he fit the cartons inside the Be Kind to Our Planet bag, put the bag under his jacket, and zipped it up for the bus ride home.

"Why, Clarence? Why did they die?"

"One needs another one."

Tom nodded. "You know your budgerigars."

"Tom, do you know bowling?"

Broken Plates

Wally made the coffee from a fresh bag of beans, but was running a little late and, without having taken his first sip, dropped his full cup. The red porcelain lay in a cracked mess on the kitchen floor.

"No!" yelled Wally.

"I'll get it," Mina said, and swiftly filled a travel mug and handed it to him. "You didn't get any on yourself, anyway. Go on. I'll wipe it up."

"I hate being late. I hate dropping things! I hate getting old."

Mina put an apple and granola bar in his other hand. "Drive carefully." Wally left the kitchen.

She picked up the big pieces and laid them on the counter, sopped up the rest with paper towels, and threw it away. Even with Wally gone, his frustrated energy lingered. She took her own coffee and the broken pieces outside.

August, already hot this morning, but she and Wally hadn't eaten a single meal outdoors all summer. After laying a clean tarp out on the picnic table, Mina retrieved a bulky bag from under her potting bench and dumped out the pieces of dishes, cups, and bowls saved over thirty-one years. She put the pieces of Wally's red cup on top of the heap. Sparrows and finches and chickadees flitted to the feeders, active and excited for the new day.

As Mina picked up each piece and cleaned it with a soft rag, the birds consoled her as they had, season by season, those busy days raising three boys: the endless cooking, the laundry, the groceries. Watching the birds in their tiny moments at the birdbath mimicked her half-hour gaps at the pottery wheel, running to short classes here and there, borrowing bits of time at friends' kilns, and entering a few pieces in small group shows. Later, her feather-imprinted plates got noticed in bigger shows; she installed her own basement kiln and now supplied a list of regular clients online.

Mina folded over one edge of the canvas, rolled the clean pieces up in it, and moved it over to the lawn. The overlarge bowl had originally been part of a fountain, salvaged from Wally's parents' place. It weighed a ton. She had positioned it, with the help of all three teens, on a circular patio left over from a cast iron fire cage she no longer wanted (the smoke rose directly into the master bedroom above). The birdbath, as they now called the old fountain bowl, was big enough to curl up in. Their youngest, Sam, used to hose it out on the hottest, most humid days, fill it to the brim, and float with his legs sticking out. The paint on the bottom, a midnight blue, eventually began to crack, and pieces of the interior concrete crumbled off with it.

Mina unrolled and spread out the tarp on the grass. She strapped on some knee pads and brought over a tray of glue and a few kids' paintbrushes. It felt good to move, sing if she wanted, make a big mess. Mina had to tiptoe around

Wally's moods, his appetites, his temperature level, even. It was worse since Sam moved out. Wally was drinking more, especially at night when she worked in the basement. He rarely came down to her workshop. He was often put off by her pottery, her studio, the time she spent there. Her work puzzled him, she suspected, as much as his habits sometimes bothered her.

She swept out the cavity of the birdbath. More chunks of aggregate plunked out onto the patio. Wally was worried about retiring, when she was only getting started. Mina fully appreciated that Wally helped build her kiln, but he only did it because she convinced him that it would someday make a profit. He, like her own father, never used the word, "art," never mind "art school." Mina wondered why they felt it necessary to quantify an activity to a dollar value. If it kept her sane, wasn't that enough? If it meant something to her, didn't that count?

Her pottery was popular. But once, when she needed a cash infusion for materials, Wally said, "You can always have a bake sale." Mina had relayed that to each of her sons, and they agreed that the comment was demeaning, promised her never to say it to their own partners or to any woman, and all offered to pitch in a hundred bucks. Instead, she took the money out of savings and replaced it later. She was looking for a moment to ask Wally to take over the business part, which completely bored her. Maybe then he'd regard her work seriously. She had to force herself to do her accounts. She was supposed to do it today—long overdue—but none of it mattered right now. Not with this undone concave mosaic demanding her, all of her, today.

She began with midnight blue, from a coffee mug, in the centre, which matched the original paint underneath. With a paintbrush, she thickly daubed glue into a pitted spot and brushed glue on the back of the blue piece, then pressed it down and held it there firmly. She remembered that blue, the freedom they felt when she and Wally moved out of their parents' houses and into that spartan apartment downtown. Their first pair of coffee mugs, lifted from the communal laundry room. Over the years, in their starter home they never left, boys dropped cereal bowls, she dropped plates, and Wally dropped cups, all completely normal. None of them had hurled the porcelain across the room, like in some of her friends' lives: volcanic marriages, seething hatred, and ring-throwing fights. That hadn't happened here, in this house they'd bought after years of saving and hoping. But other things had, periods of time that perplexed her, plagued her, even, that needed smoothing out at her potter's wheel before she could face anyone again.

She spread out the puzzle pieces of her family, her life, right side up on the tarp. A kaleidoscope. She didn't group by colour or size, preferring to let her hands do the selecting, picking each piece by feel, by instinct, intuition. Mina had long ago decided they'd eat off of mismatched dishes gleaned from garage sales. Then it didn't matter if they broke. Wally had to leave the room if he dropped anything, if it broke or even if it didn't. He must have been severely punished by his mother, a woman Mina had never met, who died right before they were married. Wally said, so she didn't have to come to the wedding. His mother's English bone china went to Wally's sister, Shauna. Mina was so relieved.

Wally was an air traffic controller. When she met him, she supposed he was calm guy with a job like that. And he was, at work, according to his workmates, who nicknamed him The Wall.

Mina rebroke the red cup that Wally had dropped this morning to make it fit next to some lime green. This cup had little airplanes on it. Maybe, she thought, dropping dishes was like dropping planes to Wally, mini-metaphors for disaster because the planes he controlled were full of people.

She held up a tangerine half-plate and found the other half. A split down the middle, like two sides of the moon. She could glue them side by side or separate them, which is what she did, tilting them suggestively toward, but not touching, the other. Working from the inside to the outside perimeter, she eyeballed the number of pieces she had for the amount of space to fill. She might not have quite enough and considered how many chipped plates lay in the kitchen cupboard. No need to replace them with only two at the table now. She stood, stretched, and went in for the extra shapes, colours, and sizes she needed and a hammer.

Mina smiled. Breaking the red one and the yellow one felt so good, but she had to wonder why, when she herself was in the "business" of making dinnerware. Because, she decided, she was making something else with them. A giant bowl of plenty, showing the efforts of love over the entire lifetime of her sons, a story bowl. She thought of the podge, white like glue but clear when dry, to smooth the surface, leaving no pokey places in case one of her (hoped for) future grandchildren took a (supervised) dip in the big birdbath.

She thought of these unknown, uncertain little children all the time now. None of the boys were actually married. None were ready for kids of their own. Their partners were all ambitious, bright young women. And Mina never brought it up; she knew better than that. She had been surprised by her yearning after all the boys had left Wally and her to themselves. She had visions of these children. So far she'd dreamed up eight. That was maybe excessive, but she'd fashioned eight distinct clay dream kids, full figures standing like the terra cotta warriors of China, about a foot high, and placed them on her basement windowsill to gaze at the stars. The door to her workshop was usually closed, but she'd left it open lately, an invitation.

Mina placed the last pieces at the rim of the giant bowl. The work had taken all day. Mina stopped for lunch but not after that, even for the phone, and her stomach was growling, her haunches sore from alternately kneeling, squatting, reaching. Once again she had completely forgotten about what was for dinner. Tuna out of the tin would be fine for her. Wally, though, expected more. Well, she thought, not tonight. It would be a brilliantly warm evening, despite the wind picking up, and she wanted to get the podge on before she quit so the birdbath would be dry tomorrow. She could hardly wait to fill it up, see the water swirl the colours, float a few gerbera daisy heads.

After she'd finished, there were four curvy cup pieces left, including one red one from the morning. Mina stored them back in a bin under her potting table in case the birdbath ever needed repair. With a big brush she lathered on the podge, "putting lots on" as her father had always advised whenever she painted his fences, his furniture, the practical objects of his life. He'd wonder why on earth she'd spend a whole day on a project like this. She cleaned up her brushes, put away the pots of glue and podge, and stood, wobbly with hunger, examining her work, pulling off her thin latex gloves, considering another coat of podge in the morning and the sealant she'd need to buy.

She heard Wally's car pull in the garage, his door closing, and another door closing.

"Hey, hon," he called as he closed the garage door. Hon, his word for "Forgive me?". He continued only when she looked back at him, silently acknowledging his apology. "You didn't answer the phone so I brought pizza and wine. Thought you must have been working and not heard."

"Come here," Mina said. The pizza, Hawaiian, was his preference, and the wine, Pinot Grigio, hers. She stood away from the bird bath so he could see.

"Wow," he said. "You saved all this?" He bent down, laid the pizza on the ground, and ran his knuckle over a piece of his red airplane cup. "It's made out of … us."

The colours were bright, like the plates she scrounged, bold and beautiful. They swished, they clashed, they flowed.

Mina shook out the tarp for pizza without plates, wine without glasses, to sit and contemplate the birdbath: their past, their now. Wally put a personal slice of pizza on a leaf for the wasps, well away on the fence. Mina picked a handful of arugula from the garden to decorate the pizza.

The mosaic pieces brought back the time the boys made dinner for their tenth anniversary and dropped six plates trying to set the table; the antique cake plate that slipped out of her hands and cracked in three but Wally's birthday cake was salvaged in one lopsided chocolate lump from off the floor; the tea cup she dropped when her water broke and they rushed to the hospital for the birth of Sam. They munched and sipped through memories, laughing and tearing up, and by the time they went in from the night breeze, for the first time that summer, they looked at each other with longing.

The Return

Ten years ago, Molly left her baby on Shauna's doorstep. Molly's baby, the same age as Jess, refused to suckle when Shauna tried to breastfeed her, turned her weak little head away from warmth, from singing, from eye contact. Shauna had never felt rejection like this; a three-month-old baby, her namesake, undid her. She bathed her, tried bottled breast milk and then formula to no avail while Peter rocked Jess and put the boys to bed. On his professional advice, Shauna took the babe to emergency. The resident obstetrician spat out exactly what Molly had said.

"Failure to thrive."

"So, what, we wait for her to die?"

"I'll order IV fluids for now and see what transpires."

Shauna wished that Peter, in his practiced hopeful manner, could talk sense into this resident. But by now, her husband was asleep. She calculated when to go home so he could get to the hospital on time for morning rounds. She hoped Jess would sleep through the night, as she had for the past week, and not disturb him.

The nurses called the baby Shauna X. The X looked like a death warrant to Shauna. She pleaded with the ICU nurse.

"But babies can recover so quickly."

"Some do, some don't. No matter what we do."

Shauna kept her hand on the babe, through a portal on the incubator, through the small hours, willing the baby to live. The tiny child slept on, barely breathing. Never cried. A little ghost. From time to time, Shauna picked her up and sang to her, even though the nurse warned against overstimulation, as if the beepers and buzzers in the unit weren't already a barrage.

The baby's interstitial IV fattened up her twig wrist with fluid. The nurse prepared to do it on the other arm. Shauna pulled out her phone from her back pocket and snapped a photo of the child lying on her back at the same moment the nurse poked the baby's arm. Shauna could hardly wait to pick the baby up, more to soothe herself than the infant, who didn't even whimper. The diaper remained dry all night. The IV alarm kept beeping.

In the photo, the baby's eyes flayed open from surprise, not fear or pain or desire. Her hair, dark, straight, and thick like Molly's. Her skin, lighter. Her eyes didn't ask a thing.

And again, the IV failed. Shauna's phone alarm sounded at six while a trio of nurses crowded the incubator to try and reinsert the IV into veins like spider webbing.

In the parking lot, Shauna felt terrible that she didn't get to say goodbye to the baby or whisper in her ear that she'd be back later.

Peter hurried out the door as she drove up, kissed her quick, and promised to look in on the babe. Shauna tiptoed in the house, downed water, and fed a hungry Jess without waking the others. It was an uneasy peace, broken when she turned Jess to the other breast. Shauna felt a loosening. A leaf falling from a tree. A feather. As soon as Jess went down for her morning nap, Shauna called the hospital.

"We were about to call you. Shauna X passed away about 0700 hours."

The nurse took her name and number in case the police needed to call. Shauna looked at her phone photo many times that day, unable to immerse herself in her own children's little needs and desires. She cried on Peter's shoulder that night.

"There was nothing anyone could do," he said. "And you did everything you could." Then quieter, he said, "When I lose a patient, I turn to sponge."

The effects of that night trickled through the years. Shauna's wish to get pregnant again required a painful reversal of Peter's vasectomy. Several miscarriages, each one sadder than the last, loaded Shauna with guilt and fear in the form of more weight. She never did go back to work, citing her own children's needs over the patients she counselled, and busied herself with the kids' activities. The array of her responsibilities at the children's schools, at church, and in the community multiplied. She took on more and more, needing to prove to herself that she could help. She ate junk food on the run and left frozen heat-up items for her family. Peter began to bake to satisfy his sweet tooth, and now whenever Shauna opened the fridge, a cheesecake beckoned. Shauna never fried hamburger again, not after it left the house reeking of burnt meat the day she took Molly's baby out of the gym bag under her mailbox.

For ten years Shauna had scanned the gatherings at church, looking for Molly at the food bank, the rummage sales, or coffee parties after services. For ten years, the plaster owls on the old brick building glared down at her in reproach.

Footsore from the third funeral luncheon this month, the guests and her team of kitchen helpers long gone, counters and sinks bleached, Shauna inhaled the chilled fall air. As she looked up at the owls, her eye caught an eagle circling high up, his spirals in the azure, his focus and grace. On her third loud wide inhale she pulled back her neck, also sore, then choked, because there was Molly, waiting under the blazing amur maple on the path to the lone car in the parking lot.

Molly wore a loose braided up-do, a knee-length tiny print dress, and faded indigo jean jacket. A tattoo on one calf, floral, continued out of sight up her leg. She stood taller, less waif-like than Shauna remembered. And she was pregnant.

If Molly seemed more solid, Shauna felt matronly: thickened waist, bulged hips. Extra pounds had slowed her down, put her in flat shoes, wide black pants, long neutral tunic tops and bold gold jewelry. Plus, her hair was falling out. She wondered if Molly would recognize her. Shauna approached Molly, surrounded by scarlet leaves.

"You look so healthy, Molly. You look great."

Molly searched Shauna's face, the big glasses, big earrings, big bust. "Is that you?"

Shauna knew that Molly couldn't say her name, and neither could she in this moment.

"Can we sit on the steps?"

Here they were, on the steps again, Shauna thought. She eased herself down on the top one where her broad bottom would at least fit. Then moved over to make room.

Molly held the railing and her belly, and settled down in the spot Shauna left for her, letting her bare legs absorb the autumn sun's warmth.

"Ah, that feels good. The doctor said don't stand if you can sit. Did you have any more kids?"

Shauna could only shake her head.

"Me neither, until this. Getting married in two weeks. Baby's coming in six."

"Congratulations."

"Todd's a long-haul driver. We have a trailer and his job is steady, five years now, and he made me quit mine because his own mom worked herself to death."

Todd, angle-parked, windows open, waited in front of the church.

"Where did you work?"

"A restaurant. Washing dishes. But one day they were short, so they put me in the kitchen, chopping and cleaning up. I learned. It fed me. Todd likes my cooking." Molly waved at him. "Been three years." He waved back. "Todd and me, both of us never grew up with a father but he's going to be the best. He calls me every day when he's away."

Todd's truck wasn't new, but it was clean, not lifted and chromed up like the one Shauna's son wanted. "Fix You" by Coldplay was audible but not ear-bashing like her middle child, the closet smoker, liked it. Molly listened to the song, too, before she spoke again.

"Your girl, did she grow up good?"

Shauna nodded. "Jess." Shauna could not bear to fill in the silence after her daughter's name. Not with her likes (all water sports) and dislikes (cats because they ate birds) or her hopes (to be a heart surgeon like her father). Molly waited until Shauna looked at her, then asked.

"Mine died, right?"

"The next morning. I tried. Everyone did." Shauna had rehearsed this moment so many times. She knew her eyes would submerge. But she didn't count on Molly putting her arm around her.

"I've been talking to her all these years. Trying to mourn her right. They said I was unfit, she was a failure. I tell her I did the best I could. She's not a failure, because she's with me always, in my heart, with my mother and grandmother." Molly's other hand alighted on her heart like a bird, then massaged her round belly. "But I'm scared."

Shauna hugged Molly to her. The baby kicked.

"Oh! I felt that!"

Shauna pulled her phone out of her purse. "I need to give her back to you." She tapped in Molly's number and sent the photo she had transferred from each of her phones to the next over the last decade.

Already, Shauna felt lighter. She so wanted to get rid of the extra pounds she carried. She visualized herself three months after Jess was born, already back to pre-pregnancy clothes, walking toward the front porch where Molly waited with her baby in a gym bag. Nothing had been the same since Shauna opened that door.

Molly took out her own phone, opened the text and stared at the photo, caressing it with thumb and finger to enlarge it.

"Her eyes. How did you get her eyes to open? I forgot how dark." Molly cradled her phone against her neck. "I couldn't—I didn't know what to do. Oh, my girl. I couldn't watch her go."

"I know." Shauna was grateful that she had not been there, either. They were both silent again. A checkmark of geese overhead honked away in a hurry. Shauna saw that Todd looked up, too.

Molly's face was wet, rumpled, deflated. Regret and fear carved her young strong face, distorted it with grief. Shauna breathed deep.

"Can I take your hand?"

Molly reached for both Shauna's hands and held tight. Shauna lowered her eyelids.

"You're at home, with Todd and the baby."

"It's a boy. We're outside."

"It's spring. There's enough sun to warm your face." Shauna paused, using her old technique to let Molly make her own picture.

"Todd holds the baby. I pour some water out by the trailer. I dig in my old parka pocket. Still there."

Shauna wondered what, and waited.

"I pat them in the dirt."

"Seeds?"

"Your tall flowers. Yellow. For her."

Shauna and Molly opened their eyes to each other.

Molly took out a card with hand-drawn sunflowers on it. "I hope you will come. The party is at the restaurant. Bring your girl, Jess?"

Shauna followed Molly down the steps to the truck. Todd jumped out and shook Shauna's hand.

"I hope to see you at the wedding," he said.

"Come visit in the spring," said Molly.

The whole way there, small black birds appeared either side of the highway in singles, then in pairs, then mating pairs and pairs in flight, black as the seeds she carried in her purse. Shauna wondered if they welcomed her or warned her.

Shauna steadied herself with self-talk. *Don't drive and visualize!* she used to say to her clients. She'd been seeing an old colleague for therapy. The volunteer work and the pounds had started to drop one by one over the winter. Walking the ravine with the dog became routine. She enjoyed cooking again, her old favourites, including dishes with hamburger.

She would ask her colleague for a part-time tryout position when she was ready. As she followed the little black birds, Shauna breathed in and out, prepared herself for what Molly needed today. And what she needed.

Todd was waiting at the trailer park entrance and guided her to their lot. He showed Shauna flat white stones the colour of bone that he'd collected by the river and circled around a freshly-dug area on the sunny side of the trailer.

Molly came down the steps with her boy. "I'm glad you came," she said. "Here's our Curtis."

"He's beautiful, Molly," said Shauna, who thumbed his round face, hugged the packed muscly weight of him. She kissed his stand-up hair.

Molly went in again and returned with still-warm rinse water and carefully set the basin down. Todd held Curtis while the women sunk to their knees and fingered a cluster of dimples in the soil. Molly put an old seed and a fresh seed in each and Shauna lightly sprinkled dirt overtop. They fisted the earth down with their knuckles, scooped water from the basin with both hands and gently pooled it in each depression. When they were done, Shauna looked up at Todd and the baby.

Overhead, geese honked their way home in the big sky.

Sunset Travel for Single Seniors

After her Oscar died mangled in the wheels of his tractor last spring, Oscar's brother Frank came over like always. Although Frank had taken meals with Violet for twenty years, usually the only sound he made at the table followed a swallow of her crabapple cider, "aahh." Tonight, Violet added candles to the table to comfort herself.

Frank hardly looked up. While he carved his marinated flank steak, Violet let loose about her daughter and son going through marital separations at opposite ends of the province. Frank was the ideal audience because he never interrupted. He took a second helping of scalloped potatoes as Violet, making the candles fan and flicker, got going.

"If they'd stayed put after they married and had me to help out, they would not be considering divorce at all. And will they bring the grandkids to Red Deer anymore? When they were all here for Oscar's funeral, I never noticed any difficulties. They ate and slept well and really, Frank, what more can we ask for? Now they're both living apart. The cost must be crazy. They're spending their inheritance on divorces. Nothing like this happened until they got their cheques last summer. Personally, I think teachers have too much time off. If they worked year-round, they wouldn't be plotting to get out of their marriages."

Frank took more garden beans.

"It's so good to have you to talk to, Frank."

She wanted to pat his hand. To her surprise, Frank patted hers. Frank could read her silence. She wondered if he could read her mind.

A shy eighteen, she had stood maid of honour for Frank and Edna. Frank asked her to dance, her soft moist hand in his great rough steady one. When he moved her to the swelling music, she in her pink dress and ivory jacket, Violet grew up all in a moment. Her heart sprung open, ready for love. She bloomed. A candle lit for the first time.

"You're going to break a heart one day, Violet," Frank whispered.

Violet, grateful that he didn't use his full voice so his comment reached her and only her, cherished it.

Then Frank handed her off to his brother Oscar.

"Where have you been all my life?"

"I feel like I've just been born," Violet said, contained in Oscar's arms.

That June night, thirty-seven years ago, remained magic. Although she had fallen for Frank, Oscar was the best man. There was no other way to stay close to Frank.

But ever since Edna died on the operating table in a botched delivery that also took their only and late-conceived infant, Frank had turned inward. He rarely spoke in those twenty years. Oscar had discussed farm matters at the table when he was alive, but now Violet carried the supper conversation. She prickled over the butcher's wife, who slid up her beef prices after the Mad Cow crisis. Considering Frank had been a rancher and he still had all his own teeth, choice meat remained Violet's most extravagant expenditure. Good thing Frank was out of the business. After so many drought years, ranching was like asking for a heart condition.

Frank went on buttering Violet's home-baked bread as the oven timer chimed the pie golden brown ready. Violet let it ding. Frank did not react. She doubted that his relatively large ears heard anything at all.

His eyes often stared off, his face turned away from her confessions—as if gazing at a sunset. Violet always assumed he dreamed about Edna. Violet missed her sister, too. Yet Violet never pined for Oscar. He had provided well, but would be unconcerned about the children run amok and five grandkids in unstable circumstances in Grande Prairie and Lethbridge. And leave it to Violet to solve, as he did any other non-farm problem, like leaky faucets, loose doorknobs, or sex.

She made the tea and cooled the pie on the sill. Violet would never barge in on her children's messy lives, especially now, but she wanted to travel, explore the world. But how, with foreign languages and currency? What was needed was a travelling partner, and it wouldn't hurt if that person were a man. Who wanted to get bothered by the Latin element? Then there were the purse snatchers. She longed to ask Frank to be her companion to Europe or Egypt or, dare she, the Taj Mahal temple of love.

Frank moved to the chesterfield for a lie-down, his habit after a satisfying supper. He picked up a brochure from Sunset Travel for Single Seniors. She'd left it open, enticingly, to the Italian Alps. She, at fifty-five, qualified, and so did Frank, at sixty-two.

They could take a tour but later break off from the group, be free of any timetable and wander. Lips might flap, but so what? But how to ask Frank? A letter was too formal, like a contract, and Violet had no time for lawyers after what they pried out of Oscar's once decent-sized estate.

If Frank would see a doctor about his hearing, then she could discuss her plan with him. Violet thought of putting something in Frank's stew to make his stomach upset enough to go to Emergency, but she dismissed that idea as a waste of fine beef.

Since Oscar died, Frank fixed the fence or mended Violet's cupboard as was his pleasure before a hearty meal. The night he worked on her rain barrel, Violet was transferring gravy to a boat when Frank hurried in to run water over his hand. Violet turned off her oven and stove.

"That's a deep cut." She wrapped it with a clean dishtowel and made him elevate his hand. "I'm taking you to the clinic." She pulled him by the elbow to her car.

Frank growled. "Uh-uh."

"It's going to need stitches. And a tetanus shot."

After the hand was stitched up, Violet asked the doctor to please look in Frank's ears. The doctor showed Frank the otoscope, demonstrated what she would do with her own ear, and then investigated his.

"Balls the size of marbles." She instructed Violet on how to melt the wax.

Frank looked worried. Violet firmly took his sinewy arm without the hurt hand and led him to the pharmacy.

That evening, Frank ate his overdone prime rib with a tilted head to keep the drops in the right ear. Before serving the rice pudding, Violet put cotton balls in that ear and Frank tilted the other way. While he reclined on the couch, Violet flushed out the melted wax from both ears with the water bulb. After the fourth day of eardrops and warm water, Violet clapped her hands behind Frank's head. Frank startled, then smiled. And began to talk in that dark rummy voice.

"Violet, what have I missed?"

"Oh, Frank. Never mind. Let's look ahead, not back."

"That's all right by me. Except to say that was a tasty roast duck tonight, Violet."

Her name again. Nothing enraptured her more.

"I look forward to tomorrow," he said.

But he didn't go to Violet's the next night or many after because when everyone found out about Frank talking again, naturally they invited him over. They lined up as if for the sphinx, to hear his resonant voice. He told stories about his ranch, played cards at the seniors' centre, and sang in the church choir. The ladies trilled at his bass under their soprano. Violet took to phoning Frank to tell him what was on for supper. If he had other plans, she put the meat back in the freezer and opened a tin of soup.

Frank went in to get his stitches removed by the same doctor.

"Frank, when was your last physical?"

"Not since after I married."

His bridge game wasn't for another hour so he let her take his pulse and pressure and order a few routine tests.

He joked, "Am I fit for love?"

"Are you thinking of remarrying?"

"I'd sure like to dance again."

"We better have a listen to your heart, then."

The doctor counselled Frank to live his life. There was not much to be done but to keep a healthy diet and exercise.

"The choir singing, especially."

Frank called Violet right away.

"Vi, what's on tonight?"

Only Edna had ever called her Vi. Her nickname in Frank's voice raced to her heart and kindled there. For the second time in her life, she felt Frank open her up to new potential, but the flame was now fire.

After a hurried mental scan of her freezer, "Sweet and sour ribs," she said.

"Can't resist your ribs. I'll be over early to finish that rain barrel."

"I better get cracking. See you soon, Frank."

"Bye, Vi."

Violet's haste heated up her own kitchen. For a little extravagance, Violet added saffron to the rice and hot peppers in the sweet and sour. For dessert, to counteract the heat in the main, lemon meringue pie from scratch. She made it right after getting the ribs in so it could set and chill.

Violet held the back door open. "Thanks, Frank. Grand to get that job done. Summer's going to be a hot one."

"I hope not another drought year." Frank dried his big hands, the scar pink.

He had dug her garden last year after the funeral. His hand was healed now, so she could ask, but what if she let the earth go fallow this year? The corn, millet, and sunflowers already poking up from the winter birdseed, couldn't they take over? Maybe he'd fixed the rain barrel for nothing.

Frank sat. "Violet." He said full her name with all the lushness it contained. "I've been thinking about a little trip this fall."

She almost dropped the casserole dish of spicy ribs on the table before sinking to the chair. Her oven mitts fell to the floor, her hands to her knees, and her eyes to Frank.

"All year I've been reading your travel magazines and, well, you've given me a hankering for Europe." Here he paused, and looked at her with a kind of awe. "If you want, we could go together, two prairie grouse out for a peek at the world?"

Flattened to her chair, the air pushed out of her soft places, Violet couldn't breathe. Not yet.

For once, she was without words. Frank's hand waited on the table.

She reached out one smooth work-worn hand and he covered it with his rough scarred one. This inflated her lungs, his chest.

"I've waited the whole of twenty years," he said. "Since I lost Edna."

"Thirty-seven for me," she said, her eyes tearing. Violet was less charitable to the memory of Frank's brother, but she kept regrets about Oscar to herself.

"I suspected it. But not until Edna went, then Oscar, could I—"

"I know. The same for me." Violet had loved her sister, too. But after Edna died, Violet allowed herself to love Frank. She never let on to Oscar, but she dreamed, in private, out on her walks, a secret pebble in her shoe, loving one man and married to his brother. But after Oscar, her heart was free to go where it wanted. That's when she'd started with the travel brochures.

And suddenly she understood her own children's struggles. It was simple. They had each fallen for someone else. They had the means. They also had the guts to make changes.

And so did she. She rose from the table, pulled Frank up into a secure embrace, then a kiss that lasted so long that they had to sit down on the chesterfield, breathless.

It was some time before they dug into the sweet and sour ribs. The heat had held in the covered casserole. The extra spice made them hungry for more. They forgot about the pie until three in the morning, propped up by many pillows, and ate directly from the pie plate with one fork.

"Before your hearing came back, when you gazed off to the corner, Frank, what were you thinking about?"

"I was trying to hear what you said. My ear to your face."

The August morning of their departure, the taxi arrived minutes early.

"He's here," Violet called to Frank in the basement.

Violet hurried to rinse the breakfast dishes. Frank turned off the main water tap, and checked the timer light.

"Did you close the bedroom doors?"

"Yes, Frank." Violet loved how thorough and practical he was.

"And unplug all the lamps and appliances?"

She enjoyed the call and return between them.

"I did the toaster and the coffee machine and the rest last night, dear." She'd taken to calling him dear as if he were her thirty-seven-years-long spouse.

"I'll take one more look around upstairs. I may have left the bedroom window open."

He loves fresh air, Violet thought as he ran up the stairs. The mountain air of the Alps and the castled valleys of the Rhine would be their first trip of many. She gathered her purse and house key and waited for Frank at the front door. After he came out, puffing a little, she double-locked the door.

"Here we go, Frank."

He carried their two suitcases down the walk as the driver opened the trunk. But after lifting Violet's small case and his even smaller one in, Frank was sweating. He held his chest, got himself into the taxi beside her, and Violet knew. The pink was leaving him, turning his skin ash grey. She redirected the taxi driver.

To Frank, she said, "We're going to fix this."

"I'm sorry, Vi." Pain distorted his voice.

Violet hushed him and told him to hang on. She kept calm, for him, but her insides had fallen into a canyon.

Frank managed to whisper with the same arousing intimacy as when they danced the very first time, "Go, Violet, and tell me all about it."

Then he blacked out, before Violet could pray or promise anything. The sound she made came from a pit under a cliff.

The taxi driver did his best to get to the hospital in time and admonished himself for not lifting the suitcases.

"He never would have let you," Violet cried, and held Frank to her.

Violet buried Frank in the plot beside Edna. An empty space waited for her in between Frank and Oscar. At home, she stared at her weeds, grieved for Frank, and listened to her hollowed out heart.

Weeks later, she softened toward the lady doctor, whom she blamed for Frank's demise, but who had cried into a tissue at Frank's funeral service as Violet left the front pew with her son and daughter supporting each arm.

Violet went in for a complete physical.

"Violet, you're fine. Better than fine, for your age."

The doctor encouraged her to do whatever she wished.

Frank's phrase, "before we die," rolled like rocks inside Violet's heart.

Sunset Travel for Single Seniors offered her credit for her trip and Frank's, both paid on her card. A week later, she booked in on a cancellation to India. Twice as expensive as Europe, but she had enough credit in her account. Frank had left his estate entirely to Violet. Frank's lawyer, a young tenor in the choir, let her sob on his shoulder and asked her to send him a postcard.

"The trip of a lifetime." She pressed Frank's words over her heart whenever it hurt.

With a thermos of ginger tea and a sandwich, Violet knelt on a tasseled aubergine pillow at Frank's graveside in an open corner of the cemetery on the outskirts of the city. She wore an amber caftan that rippled in the constant wind across the dry prairie grass. Violet assembled a vase with giant gold and orange marigolds.

"Frank, if it wasn't for our summer of love, I never would have gone anywhere. Your hand in mine. How easy we were together, after we touched. Like anything in the world was possible."

Under a rambling bit of scrub brush, a pair of grouse scrapped at the ground. Violet tossed them the crusts of her tomato and sardine sandwich. They gobbled up the unexpected prize.

As do we all, Violet thought.

Violet needed to pack for the Nile and the great pyramids of Egypt. She held the marigolds to her nose, then placed them in the shelter of Frank's headstone and picked up her pillow.

The Teeny Tiny Woman

Stooping to pick up a green apple that rolled out of the bin, Mrs. Fisher looked at Zoë eye to eye. Mrs. Fisher was older than anyone Zoë knew. Zoë sucked on her mitten string and kept hold of her mother's hand. Her mother put down her shopping basket and laid her arm gently around the woman's shoulder.

"Mrs. Fisher, how are you? And your son?"

"Oh, bless you for remembering my name. That was a long time ago we worked together. I enjoyed those days, busy in the office."

"Before I had kids. An eternity ago."

Zoë held her mother's hand tighter as she peeked at the son. She wondered how a teeny tiny woman like Mrs. Fisher could have a son as big as him. He lay in a wheelchair with the back partly down like her old stroller. Zoë's brothers used the stroller for their newspapers because it had big wheels that drove even in snow. Mrs. Fisher carried applesauce, bananas, and white bread in the crook of her arm. Zoë's mother had pink candles, eggs, and icing sugar in her basket. Mrs. Fisher turned to Zoë again.

"Are you the youngest? Is it your birthday soon?"

Zoë nodded and held up one hand with all five fingers poking up and extracted her other hand to add one more finger.

"You're a big girl now."

"I'm in Grade One."

Mrs. Fisher and Zoë's mom talked some more, Zoë silent as the big son. He had a blanket over him, red with a black stripe at the bottom. It covered even his feet. She put her hand on it, and it was as scratchy as it looked. Around his neck hung a bib made out of a dishtowel. Zoë sounded out the words on it, "Vi-va Las Ve-gas." Mrs. Fisher wiped her son's chin with the bottom of the towel, one gentle swipe in the middle of her sentence.

"We manage. As long as I can get to the store. I bring Ben so I don't slip." She touched his cheek and then a sunshine smile came out and then a cloud moved over. His face went from crunched up to smooth to crunched up again. Mrs. Fisher and Zoë giggled at each other with their eyes. Zoë's mom picked up her shopping basket and followed Mrs. Fisher to the cashier.

"You be sure to call me if you need us to run to the store for you. Zoë and I could do that. And soon, Zoë can do it on her own."

Zoë looked up at her mom, surprised. Her mom took her hand again with a little squeeze. Zoë squeezed back.

Mrs. Fisher paid for her groceries from a little change purse she pushed back down into her pocket, then patted Zoë's cheek. Zoë pulled away. A frozen leaf. The hand that touched Ben, that wiped away his drool.

"Sorry. I have such poor circulation now. Another reason to get out and walk. Plus, it's almost spring. A grand day."

"You're amazing, Mrs. Fisher," said Zoë's mother. "You and Ben look very well."

"Ben holds the groceries for me." She lifted up the blanket. Ben wore red-striped pyjamas and a navy blue bathrobe. After hooking the plastic bag of groceries under his curled up hands, Mrs. Fisher tucked the red blanket back under his chin. Now he had a Santa belly. Zoë reached up and patted it, still hanging on to her mom, but Ben didn't light up again. Mrs. Fisher did up her coat tight at the neck, pulled her scarf up over her head and tied it with a snug knot, and got her mitts back on.

"Every day, there's something good that happens. Right, Ben? Today we met you." Ben kind of clucked his tongue. Mrs. Fisher let out all her air to start the long wheelchair moving.

She turned as the automatic door opened for her and waved, "Happy Birthday, Zoë."

Ben said, "Ha-bee."

"Bye, Ben," Zoë said.

A man coming in the store helped Mrs. Fisher turn the lying down wheelchair toward home. Zoë looked up at her mom.

"How old is that teeny tiny woman?"

"She must be eighty," said her mother. "Every time I see her, I wish I'd gone around to check on her. She only lives a few blocks away from us, on the way home from the store."

"We could take some birthday cake."

"If there's any left. We should."

"Does she feed Ben like a baby?"

"She does now. He's her baby again."

The cashier, whose nametag said Brenda, smiled at Zoë and offered her a sucker. Zoë took a green one, but put it in her pocket for after because she wanted to carry the groceries, too, like Ben. She stuffed her hands in her mitts and put one arm under the bag because of the eggs, and held them to her belly. Mrs. Fisher and Ben were already gone.

"There they are," said Zoë. Down the side street, two boys playing street hockey pushed Ben's wheelchair up a wooden ramp to a little pink house while Mrs. Fisher opened the door. Zoë watched the boys come back out of the house, pick up their sticks, and chase after the puck.

While they waited at the big road with the lights, Zoë changed arms but wouldn't take her mother's hand.

"I'm practising doing it by myself." She dangled the bag and Zoë's mother put her hand on her shoulder anyway as they crossed the street. Zoë carried the groceries the whole way home, three blocks.

"How many eggs do we need?" Zoë asked.

"Four, but let's use six!"

Inside the kitchen, Zoë carefully set the bag on the table and ran to wash her hands with soap before her mom could say it, so she could crack the eggs for the cake.

After the last girl left the birthday party, Zoë inspected the chocolate cake on the dish.

"That's half of half, right?"

"A quarter. Enough for everyone to have a small slice after supper."

"Let's save half a quarter for Daddy and take the rest to Mrs. Fisher and Ben."

Zoë's mother had forgotten. "We already saw her today. I don't want to bother her now."

"Tomorrow, then." Zoë was tired out. She'd had six friends over, and the quiet felt like a blanket after the loud talking and games and presents. "Do you think Ben has naps?" Zoë used to have naps before she started kindergarten. She felt like having one now.

"Tomorrow's Sunday, and we have the boys' hockey game, and grandma for supper. We'll see."

The next day, while her parents and brothers got ready for hockey, calling out for washed uniforms and socks, looking for car keys and filling water bottles, Zoë sliced the quarter cake in half and lifted one part into a margarine container. There was still a piece left for Daddy, who was too full for cake after supper. The boys would have eaten it by now, but Zoë had hidden it overnight in the lazy Susan with all the extra pots and pans.

Zoë put the container into her knapsack along with two of the pink polka dot napkins and pink plastic forks left over from her party. She took the dog leash and called out to her mom, "I'm taking Joey for a walk."

"Okay, but only once around the block," her mom said. "We need to leave for the rink soon." Zoë spent many Sundays at the rink watching her brothers play. The rink smelled like wet wood and dirty snow and sweaty socks. She didn't like the noise, either, the yelling. So she had her own earphones and iPod in her knapsack and a few books and paper and coloured pencils. "I'm all ready," Zoë said, showing her knapsack on her back.

She walked Joey quicker than usual and he happily kept up, but pulled when she left their own block and headed down to the busy street. She wasn't allowed to cross on her own, but a lady was there waiting, and Zoë went beside her, so that wasn't alone. Joey was squirreling back and forth, not heeling at all, and almost tripped the lady. Zoë pulled his leash in tighter. After the busy road, they had to cross again to Mrs. Fisher's, so Zoë waited for no cars on the road and quickly pulled Joey across. She slipped in the slush on the other side, but didn't fall. Joey was starting to bark now, little nervous chumfs.

At the tiny pink house, Zoë walked up the ramp, way longer than the one at kindergarten. Joey heeled now, sniffing. She rang the bell. And waited. There were no boys outside playing. Maybe they were on her brothers' team and on their way to the rink. She'd have to hurry, but Mrs. Fisher took a long time to get to the door. When she did, she eyepopped at Zoë.

"Hello, Zoë. Did you walk all the way over here by yourself? Does your Mommy know?"

Before she could answer and take her pack off, Joey pulled away from her and ran in the house, chasing a small white cat. Mrs. Fisher went after him and stepped on his leash. The cat cowered on top of the lying-back wheelchair, then perched on Ben's neck.

Zoë walked in without taking her boots off like she would at school or at home because the floor was already dirty with sand, grit, and cat litter. She took Joey's leash and Mrs. Fisher picked the cat off Ben.

"Ah-ah-ah," called Ben.

"This is Snowball," said Mrs. Fisher.

"She's really cute. I'm sorry about Joey. He's nuts about cats. He likes them, but always scares them."

Zoë put her foot tight on the leash so Joey had to lie down. Ben gurgled.

"I brought you some cake, Ben."

"Ha-bee," Ben said.

Mrs. Fisher smiled wide, teeny tiny teeth in her shrunken face.

"Oh, Ben loves cake. Especially happy birthday cake. Should we have a tea party?"

"Yes! Does Ben drink tea?"

"Cooled with an ice cube, and through a straw."

"Can I have mine like that, too?"

Mrs. Fisher nodded and went to the kitchen.

In the living room, plants hogged the window. Photos and pictures and tinsel ropes were tacked up higgledy-piggledy, like her teacher said about messy printing. For Ben, Zoë thought, so there's always something for him to look at wherever he's parked. Joey was busy sniffing anything in reach. She would draw a picture of Snowball for Ben, whose eyes were focussed on the cat, now atop a bookshelf. Zoë looked around at where to sit. There was only one chair in the living room, and it was piled with books and plates and a phone, which rang, suddenly.

Mrs. Fisher hurried back in the room. "Hello? Oh, yes. She's here. The sweet darling brought us cake. Yes, I'll tell her. No trouble, not at all." To Zoë, she said, "Your Mommy will pick you up in ten minutes."

That meant they couldn't have tea, but Zoë wanted Ben to try her cake. She brought out the napkins and forks.

Mrs. Fisher put a new bib on Ben, which said Mexico, another gift from Brenda at Safeway, she explained to Zoë, who also asked about Viva Las Vegas. "She gets them on her trips. Ben travelled to Mexico and all over, before," Mrs. Fisher explained. "Then he had an accident and that's when I quit working with your mom." Mrs. Fisher rummaged and found a spoon on the chair pile.

"Forks are too sharp for Ben," she said. She wiped the spoon off on the old bib, took a bit of cake with some icing on it and handed it to Zoë. "You give it. Go ahead." Mrs. Fisher took Joey's leash.

Zoë put the spoon near Ben's nose so he could sniff it, like Mrs. Fisher said, and then he opened his mouth and closed it on the spoon.

"Do you like it?" Zoë asked.

And the cloud in his fisted face smoothed away and the sun came out again as Ben opened his eyes. Zoë laughed out loud with Mrs. Fisher.

"He likes it!"

She waited a minute like Mrs. Fisher said, and spooned another tiny piece in, making sure there was some icing. Ben looked directly at Zoë, and this time his sun smile came even before the spoonful.

The doorbell rang, and Zoë saw the van outside.

"Oh, Zoë! Don't ever do that again! I was terrified—." Then her mom looked around the room and bustled Zoë and Joey out.

"Everything's fine," Mrs. Fisher said, although she looked worried.

"If she ever does this again, phone me right away. Sorry. We have to go."

Zoë only had a chance to wave at Mrs. Fisher from the sidewalk, but not to say bye to Ben.

"I don't want to go to hockey. Can't I stay and have a tea party with Mrs. Fisher and you pick me up later?"

"No."

"Why?"

"Because."

In the van, Zoë put Joey in her lap. She couldn't take him next time because of Snowball, or maybe she could tie him up outside. Her mother looked at her as if she heard every word of Zoë's thoughts and put her hand on Zoë's arm.

"I'll go with you next time."

"I'm not a baby." I can go by myself, Zoë thought.

Her mother said, "Only if you tell me first, so I can send you with some soup for Mrs. Fisher and Ben."

But Zoë never went.

Weeks later, when Zoë walked alone to the store for the first time, to buy milk, she asked the store lady who gave her a sucker before if she'd seen Mrs. Fisher and Ben. Zoë thought she'd stop there on the way home. If Brenda offered her a sucker, she'd ask for two, one for Ben.

"Oh, they've moved, into an old folks' home."

"But Ben isn't an old folk."

When Zoë finished paying, she waited, but Brenda did not bring out her basket of suckers.

"What about Snowball? Did Snowball die?"

Brenda had already turned her happy smile to chitchat with the next customer. Zoë carefully picked up her bagged carton of milk and walked straight home like her mother asked.

That afternoon all she wanted to do was draw. Because Snowball was a white cat, Zoë could only do her outline and give her pink lips and nose, and closed eyes.

The Maternity Project

When I invite her to my baby shower, Meg can hardly say no. Meg is nineteen and new to the city and, as Mom would say, naïve as paste, like her when she had me. But Meg hops to the Dollar Store at lunch and buys decorations with her own money. Blue for a boy.

She concocts Kraft Dinner with frozen peas for my girls. Snotballs, they call them. They giggle down a few bites, even the peas, then scramble to help Meg stick blue elephants on the windows and walls. I'm about to bribe them to finish their suppers, but I'm too slow and miss my chance. Instead, I eat their leftovers, still warm, while I clear up. I spit the peas into the garburator.

Then I settle down with a tall ginger ale and ice because KD twists my gut, and put my swollen feet up. Since I moved us to the condo, I don't think I've sat down before the girls go to bed. By the time we get home from daycare, it's way past six, then supper to prep, feeding, playing, bathing, clean up, and lunches to make.

Jasmine came first, then three years later, Jola, and after another three years, here I am, an elephant with little boy blue Jae, one month till payday.

I knew Meg would ask, but at least she had the sense not to in front of Jola and Jasmine. On the subway ride to daycare after work, a knitting blue-hair slows down her tsk-tsk needles to listen, but I don't care and neither does Meg.

"Why don't you marry the fathers?"

"That's old-school."

"Why not use a sperm bank?"

"Because that costs money, and the fathers support me."

"Do they know each other?"

"Are you kidding? I let the guy brag about his finances, get pregnant on a one-nighter and then sue for child support when the baby is born. The guys set up payments to stay out of court, then head to Fort Mac. And I go on mat leave."

"So Jasmine is black, Jola is Latina, and Jae?"

"Asian. He'll be smart."

"Is that on purpose?"

"The next one will be Indigenous. Also gorgeous."

"Where do you find these guys?"

"I have a few lucky bars when I'm on the lookout."

"When you're working the system."

Seriously? We work for the government. "Do you know how much work it is to drop the baby weight and get into decent bar clothes by the time you finish breastfeeding? It motivates me to get back in shape." This is my livelihood.

But later, at home, Meg goes at me again.

"How many do you want?"

"As many as it takes." All I want to do is not work, take good care of the kids, and not worry about money. "Lots of expenses with kids and daycare and I want to take a few trips."

"Trips where, Mommy?" Jasmine says.

"Private Mommy trips. Bikini, martini, and me."

"Oh," says Jasmine. She shakes her head at Jola.

"When I get to stay home, every day will be a field trip. We'll go to the zoo and the pool and the mall. As soon as Jae is born, we get a whole year to play. No daycare."

"Can we go to the park?" That's Jola. Such simple needs.

"I can hardly wait, sweetie." I pat her head so she'll believe me.

"Nice condo, by the way. How did you finance this?" asks Meg. So young.

I send the girls squealing to get ready. They've wanted to put on their new matching balloon print T-shirts since the morning.

"Sold my eggs."

Meg blanches a little.

"The medical company flies you to San Diego once for shots, then does the extraction over a weekend so you get a little time after on the beach, and then flies you back, all expenses paid, for a big fee in u.s. dollars. More if you have a higher degree." I try to pick a time when I earn big on the dive-bombing Canadian dollar.

"Wow. Does it hurt?"

"It mostly hurts after, but they give you pain meds. I have egg-kids somewhere in California."

"Can they find you?"

"The records are sealed." Not like with my birth mom. Freaked her right out at first. She never had any other kids but me, it turns out, but she sure put on her Supergrandma motorcycle jacket for the girls.

"Would you do it again?"

"Have to. To finance a van. My car won't fit everybody after Jae moves up to a sit-up car seat. Kids have to ride in the back." After Jae is almost one and weaned, I'll go, before my mat leave is up. But this time, I'll go a week ahead. Get the tan, hair streaked, gel nails. But where to leave three kids for a week? It was going to be Mom, but Mom stroked out shovelling the snow while I was buying groceries. Mom so loved the girls. Good thing Jasmine knew how to phone me right away. The girls even dragged her inside, out of the cold.

Meg could probably handle a week of babysitting, but she'll be back at school in the fall. I go ahead and pitch it to her.

"Maybe Reading Week. February? If you want the job."

"Papers to write. But I could do it after April exams, before I start back in May. If I get rehired."

I knew I could count on Meg. "You're getting a great rec letter from me before I go on maternity." She can do her job almost too fast; it pisses off the other workers. But good for them, to see how they need to keep up. I'll suggest a special project for Meg this summer to keep her interested and a promotion and pay raise next summer to make sure she comes back. Fast learners get bored fast, need more supervision, than the regulars.

This mat leave, my main project is to find a new sitter for the kids. To go with my new neighbourhood, condo, and family of four. Meg's serious student vibes won't let me have her much during the university semester, except maybe for emergencies. I hope Jasmine and Jola will be interested in school, too, especially since Mom left all her money to them in RESPs. Good thing, because I can't save a dime. I blame that on my supervisor job in Accounts Payable, ten years now. You get a little overpaid, and you overspend, but if you do it month after month, you dive right into debt. I can't save much, but I've been debt-free for two years and I'm going to keep it that way. Mom got me straight on that and if anyone knew about debt, it was her. Starting with thirty-five years of maternal abandonment.

While I pop popcorn, Meg cuts veggie sticks and shows the girls how to stir the lemonade with the jug in the sink. After Meg vacuums, we circle the kitchen chairs in the living room, empty except for the one couch and side table. The girls like it open to play in.

We wait for the guests.

Did I make a mistake on the invitation? Even the girls' excitement wanes. They're more interested in drawing with Meg. One of the blue elephants' heads comes unstuck and flops over. I invited seven other neighbourhood moms with decent cards, gold envelopes, and blue stork stickers. The last invitation in the package went to Meg.

"Do you know the women you invited very well?"

"That's what this was supposed to be. Hello, here we are, nice to meet you." And thank you for the present. Not. This is a bust. What a waste of time. Except Meg's getting to know Jola and Jasmine. Then it hits me that the women in this community all have husbands who live in their actual condos and it's pretty obvious that I don't have one, moving all our stuff in by my pregnant self, bit by bit, with two preschoolers helping me. Is that why? Or because Jasmine and Jola obviously have two different dads? Have I landed in Redneck Crescent? Has no one here heard of Madonna? Angelina Jolie?

I wish Mom was here. She'd have had every mother all talked up and interested and happy for me and feeling generous with their shower gifts and on time for the party. While I grew up and out of foster care, Mom worked at the Flamingo Casino and could talk to anyone while taking wads of their money. "It's like Monopoly money after a while," she said. But she knew how to manipulate it. She showed me the numbers for three, then four, and five children: expenses and revenue and those two columns need to match. We'd have made such a great team. I pick up her framed photo, the one at the elephant exhibit at the zoo. I hold the photo to my heart. The girls copy me doing this sometimes but lately it's mostly me when I lie down. After a day at work this pregnant, I drop asleep like a bomb.

The doorbell wakes me. I wave to Meg, in the middle of a book with the girls, to answer the door. At this stage, after I nap my body feels like it's scooped my brain out of my skull and gone to the spa without me.

"Hello. Party here?" A short Asian lady with searching eyes bustles in and claps her hands at me flat out on the couch, like that could set my brain back in place.

Meg tries to distract her. "Um, yes. For Jae, the baby?"

But she zeroes in on me. "Yes, happy time. My son brings me. He says, you his friend."

Her little claw hands quiver, hovering over my big belly. Old ladies believe they have magic, prophetic, or fortune-telling powers and therefore, licence to feel. I snap myself up before she can touch me and sidestep to the window. The silver sports car she came in, with leather interior and fine wood detailing, waits in my driveway for a stroller mom to pass, then backs up and drives away. I'm still clutching Mom, and put her back on the coffee table, a witness.

"Mrs. Wong," I say. I must have mentioned the baby shower to Jonathan.

The woman is all over my tummy, holding it this side and that. Cornered by a dwarf who comes up to my swollen coconuts, I can hardly see where her hands are. But they're talking to me: *Your unborn son is my blood. My grandson.*

"Would you like some ice cream cake?" That's Meg.

"Yes. Party cake?" Mrs. Wong pulls my girls over to her.

"Maybe let's wait for the others," I say.

"No, no! Let's have it now," yell Jasmine and Jola.

I could take the cake back. White with blue icing but no writing, so totally returnable. Sixteen dollars.

"I cut it," says Mrs. Wong. She bulldozes into the kitchen on her own and brings back a double-sized piece and three forks.

Mrs. Wong feeds the cake to Jola with a blue plastic fork, tiny bit by bit, without dropping a crumb. She smiles and fusses. Meg takes photos and gets them up on social media. I'd like to add for all the no-show mothers, *Look what you're missing, suckers.* I should have invited all the ladies at work, but they've already come to Jasmine's and Jola's showers. I'm still hoping they might have an impromptu lunch party before I leave and maybe a gift certificate to the Bay because, you know, boys need different things. I open Mrs. Wong's gift, a velour blue sleeper. A quality one. She must have got it on sale. Yup, there's the marked-down price tag from Winners. I leave the tissue paper and ribbon on the floor to make the place look like a party. Meg gives a gift card to McDonalds. Very original.

"The girls can play in the PlayPlace and give you and Jae a quiet feeding time." Okay, I buy that. Actually, pretty thoughtful. How does she even know that?

I remember to thank them both and look them in the eyes. Mom taught me. She could have taught me a whole lot more. Like how to cope without adult company. How to dream. How to plan. How to keep trucking.

"So, Jonathan is your son," I venture.

"Yes. Good boy. My son. And my grandson, so healthy. Name Jae."

I redden. My family plans do not include any contact with the fathers or their families.

"Practice grandson," she continues. "Jonathan say no more dates, eh?"

"We went out once and once was enough."

Mrs. Wong claps again. Startles me every time.

Meg gets her talking about him, Jonathan smart this and Jonathan smart that. Her only son. It's pretty nauseating, but Meg's lapping it up until Mrs. Wong makes it clear that only a Chinese girl is good enough to be her son's wife.

"But grandson, no matter who the mother. Grandson is grandson."

I extract Jola but then Jasmine climbs on Mrs. Wong's lap for her piece of cake, also hand fed, with the second fork. Like a big bird.

"Can you start the bath, Meg? Time for the girls to go to bed." They run to the tub with her.

While the water runs in the bathroom, I sit to get my eyes level with the beetle eyes of Mrs. Wong.

"You're not welcome here, Mrs. Wong. I don't want to see you again."

"I see you again. You're welcome." She takes my hand.

I pull it away. "Jonathan should not have brought you here."

"I come back by myself. For Jae. My grandson."

"I'll write this in to our agreement. Jonathan has to keep you away."

"I make wonton soup for the girls. Next time I come. You have big pot?" She bangs her way through my kitchen cupboards until she finds it. And brings it to the door. She's taking my pot home to fill up. In a dizzy moment I imagine Jae, my unborn Jae, curled in the pot, under the lid. I know it's preggo fuzzbrain, but it terrifies me.

"You can't take that. It's mine."

"Who else going to help you?" Mrs. Wong says. "That Meg, she have job, then school."

It was going to be Mom. She never told me about her lung condition. Another reason to mix my kids' genes up a bit. If I'd known Mom and I only had three years to figure each other out, I'd have looked for her sooner. I didn't get the urge until after Jola. Until I sorted out my own way to have my family, for myself.

Meg brings the kids in, ready for bed. I hold out my arms, but the girls run to Mrs. Wong.

"When are you coming back?" says Jasmine.

"I see you soon. You good girls. Best big sisters for my grandson." Jola and Jasmine each get a kiss goodnight and a squeezy hug from Mrs. Wong.

"Tuck us in?" Jola says. They each take a hand and lead her to the bedroom.

I motion for Meg to help me pick up the decorations and put them in a bag.

"You could reuse them," she says.

"Get rid of this nightmare." I squish the blue elephants into paper balls. Mrs. Wong sings to the girls snuggled in their flannel sheets.

I lock myself in the bathroom. Meg and Mrs. Wong clean up the living room, put back the chairs, and tidy the kitchen, chattering about recipes and cleaning tips and gardening. When Jonathan comes to pick up his mom, Mrs. Wong makes him drive Meg home, too. They both call out goodbye but I pretend not to hear.

"Are you sure you're okay?" says Meg. "I can't leave unless you say. You're not having premature labour pains, are you? I'm outside your door until you say you're fine."

How can she care that much about everything? "Thanks but I need some alone time." That's what I say to the kids when I lock myself in the bathroom, and it works on Meg. She and Mrs. Wong bang out the door with the big pot, dropping the lid twice and laughing.

The next weekend, I go into labour three weeks early while Jonathan is at his engineering firm barbeque. He takes my call like it's a message from his accountant, sends his mom over in a taxi to watch Jasmine and Jola, and prepays the cabbie to take me to the hospital. He also arranges for flowers when I return from the delivery room with a card that promises his mom will come over the next day with a stuffed blue elephant for Jae.

An easy-peasy birth, no problems, and Jae's a good size even being half-Asian and a few weeks premature. I miss Mom, who promised she'd be here because she wasn't at Jola's or Jasmine's births since that was before I found her. I really wanted her here for this one. I thought it would reunite us, rewrite the moment she gave me up and put me on the merry-go-round from foster home to foster home. I was too smart and nobody likes a smartass kid, but Mom says I was a survivor, like her, because we got along alone even though we thought about the other every single day. Who knew that pile of emotional splinters could ignite intense and full love at first sight?

Mom fell for my girls like she might have for me. She made every moment count. I tell Jae all about it while he feeds, in our own curtained off bubble in a quad ward of new mothers and their families. One mom I recognize from three years ago when Jola was born here. What are the odds of that? We nod, veteran moms, sore and tired and happy and facing years of responsibility with fierce pride. The other mom has a girl this time, two boys at home. No man in sight. We mirror each other. Do I look that exhausted? We exchange phone numbers but I doubt we'll ever call each other.

Mrs. Wong stays overnight like I knew she would and the girls sound happy and fine on the phone. Mrs. Wong is bringing the girls over to meet their brother and then we'll all go home for wonton soup.

Before Mrs. Wong arrives, I keep Jae with me every minute and tell him the whole story. He needs to connect with my voice before he hears hers. He really responds to sounds. He's extremely intelligent, I can tell. Brilliant, I bet. His eyes are so curious. Before he meets Mrs. Wong, I want him to see his other grandma. I show him her picture. He stares. Not cross-eyed like most newborns, but totally concentrating. Fixed on her face, and I know Mom's helping me wherever she is. Then it occurs to me that maybe she sent Mrs. Wong.

When Jae sees his Chinese grandmother, he blinks and I watch her tumble in love. And in that moment, we're the same. We're two women alive with love for a baby boy named Jae. Mrs. Wong makes me laugh, and I thank her a hundred times, for the blue elephant, the candies, the oranges, for loving Jae, too. We sink into his serene eyes.

That's when I wonder, what if something happens to me? I can't be all my kids have. Foster care is most definitely not an option, so I'm going to ask about Jola's and Jasmine's other grandmothers. As Mom would say, consolidate your resources. I asked her, why Denny, why name me that, and she said, "Denny for Denise, my mother." Even I have one little thing from a grandma I never knew.

While I struggle through post-partum cramping, which is worse this time, I push away thoughts of my three kids under six alone while I'm bleeding on a California freeway or strangled on a Mexican beach and instead imagine inviting Mrs. Wong and Mrs. Esperanto and Mrs. Walker for tea. The girls and I serve cut-out cookies we made ourselves for the very first time, and Jae lies on a blanket in the centre of the room chewing his blue elephant. A private family gathering: three ladies and the three children who share their blood. Meg's there, too, taking pictures. Mom is there, too, in her frame on the side table, smiling, always smiling. I know it's a fantasy, but it cheers me. Darn hormones.

In our agreement, Jonathan will come to the hospital and sign the documents. He'll bring the car seat. He'll drop Jae and the girls and me off at home. And take Mrs. Wong away, unless the girls share the top bunk like they did last night and Mrs. Wong keeps the bottom one, for now.

Spring Fever

With one arm, Charlie cradled the burlap bundle and, with the other, he clutched the railing down the steep steps of the bus. The heat of the afternoon hit his bare head, the sun made him squint, and he didn't see the skateboarder careening down the sidewalk toward him.

"Geezer!" the kid called out over his shoulder.

Charlie froze a moment, waiting for the other boarders. They travelled in a pack of three and used his driveway to build speed when they thought he didn't notice, but he did.

The bus puffed dust and fumes as it pulled away but still Charlie didn't move until he stood alone on the curb.

Protecting his package against his chest with both arms, Charlie began to cross the street to his tidy little bungalow when a water truck downshifted to avoid hitting him.

"Lardass," yelled the driver.

Charlie didn't hear and kept going nevertheless, not stopping until inside the haven of his garage. He unwrapped the burlap on his potting table. He snipped the tag off, $64.99, pricey but worth it for its colour, a shocking hot pink. He stored the tag in a logbook, marked the date in grease pencil, gathered his tools and a pail of high-grade fertilized mix, propped open the side door, and carried his prize out to the other rose bushes in the yard.

"Say hello to Sexy Lady. Give a warm welcome to your queen." Sexy Lady had been on special order for over a year.

Only then, he noticed. He whirled back into the garage. Sweetheart, his British racing green '72 Jaguar XKE hardtop had vanished! He hadn't even looked when he came in! He nearly dropped Sexy Lady and, when he caught her, a thorn nipped through his worn leather glove.

Hastily, he planted and watered the rose bush without the usual ritual of stalk placement, fertilizer layers, and repeated soaking. He put it in without another word to the others, situated in a spiral. This one, in the centre, finished the rosarium. He packed down the dirt roughly with his foot, pulled off his gloves, chucked his trowel (which rarely rested on the ground) outside the garage door, unhooked the triple-latched gate without even checking that it closed behind him, and ran down the street to his neighbourhood beat patrol station in the strip mall a block and a half away.

Red-faced and sweating at the front counter, he asked for Donna first.

"She quit," said the young thin thing, "said she had spring fever."

"Where's Arnie?" Charlie demanded.

"He hasn't come in yet. Late shift." Then she coloured, her crush for the genial superfit constable animating her face. "Wait, I think I hear his cruiser. Take a seat."

Charlie could not take a seat. He waited at the counter and spilled out his story before Arnie had both boots in the door.

"Whoa, Charlie." But Charlie couldn't "whoa." He usually said five words maximum at a time, but now the same story fountained over and over. After the third rendition, Arnie nodded to his new volunteer assistant and ushered Charlie out to investigate. They walked the distance to Charlie's garage, Charlie a little behind Arnie's long-legged stride.

Breathless, Charlie pushed in his code for the overhead door and up it went. And there sat his barn-find restored Jaguar, engine slightly warm.

"Guess you didn't see it the first time." Arnie grinned.

"Someone took it out. Really, Arnie. Feel the engine." Charlie, relieved to see Sweetheart intact, worried about how she'd been handled. Could it have been one of the skateboarders? Had he missed them, with his eyes shut when the bus pulled away? And with the water truck, that noise machine?

Arnie said, "I didn't even know you owned a car. And what a car." Arnie ran a hand over her rear lines the same way Charlie did the first time he saw her.

Charlie was gratified that Arnie gave the Jaguar the praise she deserved. "I keep it in case of emergency," he said.

"Or a hot date?" Arnie, still tickled, wrote down the time in his log book and left Charlie in his perplexed state.

On the way back down the street to the station, Arnie stopped in at Donna's, who waved him in for coffee. He told her about Charlie. He also remarked on her empty backyard, vacant since the old garage had come down.

"Yeah, that's my project. Planting it all in," Donna said. There were bedding plant trays filled with yellows and orange and pinks on her back porch. "When you get to my age, every spring is a gift. From now on, I'm following my heart. There should be a law about that."

"Ah, spring," said Arnie. "The kids failing school come out for a few kicks and end up in juvie, the street folks get restless, and the old guys emerge from hibernation to waste my time."

"Charlie never does that," Donna said. "He's one of your eyes and ears and you know it. Especially since Rosie went, five years now."

"I think he's losing it, Donna. Happens to everyone."

"Take some cookies for the new girl. She's way too skinny."

"Miss you, Donna. Look in on Charlie for me, would you?"

"Don't worry about him."

Arnie didn't. Donna would take care of the situation, like she had when she worked for him as a citizen volunteer every day for fifteen years. Widowed way too long. A rock of a woman, thought Arnie.

Charlie watched Arnie walk away from Donna, certain that he told her and she thought he was demented.

He fussed about that while he made a place in his Nanking cherry bushes, with a small stool to sit on, a thermos of coffee to keep him awake, camera and binoculars at the ready. Sure enough, as the rosy afternoon light spread lazily across the driveway, he woke up from a bent head snooze to glimpse Sweetheart drive away. The driver glided slowly, not haphazardly, at least. Short in the driver seat. For sure one of the skateboard kids. Charlie fed both what he knew and what he conjectured on the garage phone to Arnie. He even had photos, like a professional UFO watcher.

"Okay, Charlie. When it got back earlier, it was spic and span, not a scratch on her, and filled with gas, right? Let me know when she gets home." Arnie turned back to his reports before he hung up the phone.

The garage door gaped wide open, and the skateboarders

jumped off at the top of the driveway. One pushed the button to close the overhead door.

"No, no, no!" yelled Charlie from inside the garage and pushed the inside button to reopen it. He counted the boarders: three.

"Hey, man, we thought you forgot to close it. Can't be too careful" said the leader, the one with blond hair in a bun who had nearly creamed him earlier. "You've got tools 'n stuff in there, eh?"

"Yeah, leave it open."

"Okay, man."

"Thanks anyway."

"Old fart," the skater barked out to his pals, down the sidewalk. Charlie heard that and let some gas go in reply.

Back in the bushes, Charlie waited for what seemed like hours. The sound of the driver door gently closing woke him from a troubled dozing position, head in hands. It was already dusk. The Jaguar side-opening hatch door was open. Charlie, afraid to confront the thief, wished he'd brought a baseball bat. Shoulda, woulda, coulda, he thought.

"Throw me the key!" he yelled.

The key landed in the bush a little behind Charlie. He turned and had to take three grabs for it, caught in some undergrowth. By the time Charlie's head came out of the dirt, the intruder had fled. Charlie didn't hear running steps even though he'd changed his hearing aid batteries after the water truck incident. The boarders skated by again. The trunk of Sweetheart, splayed open, lit up a packed tray of multi-coloured pansies.

The last boarder skated by. "Hey, your honey come home?"

"Did you see who ran out of here?" called Charlie. No answer from the teen, eyes focussed on the piece of pavement ahead. Charlie was steaming mad. At himself, for not catching the perpetrator, at the car, for being vulnerable to theft, and at the thief, who had outwitted him again.

Charlie inspected the key ring. A rose with three keys: the house, garage, and car. It was a set he'd given to Rosie ages ago. Now curiosity bobbed out of perturbation. Was this a sign from Rosie? On the day he'd completed the rosarium, what she always wanted, posthumously?

In haste he stowed the stool back inside the garage, stuffed his back pockets with garden gloves in one and his smallest trowel in the other, pulled on his hat, zipped on his jacket, fetched the tray of painted pansies, closed the trunk and the overhead door and, for the second time that day, crossed the street in heated-up confusion. His face burned red.

The bunhead boarder whizzed by the other way. "Watch out, Romeo."

Charlie pushed open Donna's gate. The mechanism needed tightening. In the bare backyard, freshly rototilled, in the last of the setting sun, Donna placed a jug of lemonade on a little patio table. Two glasses.

But Charlie didn't see that, nor the blooming marigolds, zinnias, asters, and cosmos in nursery packs all over the sidewalk. He didn't even wait for Donna to turn around.

"Why did you take my Jaguar?"

"Rosie gave me the keys years ago."

In his stern managerial voice, Charlie said, "In case of fire."

Donna's voice was quiet as she fingered a blue pansy in the tray he carried. "Yeah. I got it bad."

Charlie put down the flat of pansies. "Why didn't you ask me for the car?" He never would have lent it to her anyway, and she must know that. "Or ask me to drive you to the greenhouse?" Even though the bus went right there.

"To get your attention."

Charlie wondered how much Donna and Rosie had talked. Since Rosie passed, he had admonished himself for having spent all his free time with Sweetheart, restoring her from near-ruin when he acquired her at an incredible price twenty years ago. Yet Rosie never seemed to mind. They'd had no children, but Rosie had her groups, her friends, her activities, and he had work at the gas company and Sweetheart. Why had he picked that name? At Donna's tentative smile, it hit him.

"Spring fever," he and Donna said at once, then laughed, young again, together.

His face relaxed as he considered the expanse of soft soil to be planted. The trays of blooms. Donna, waiting. The sun lingering. The kitchen window, and the aroma of meatloaf in the oven. The lemonade.

Charlie pulled out his worn gloves and his trusty trowel. "Let me give you a hand with these."

The Red Velvet Curtain

At the next full moon circle of wives on the range road, Maura wished for it to be over, so she could drive home and walk up to the lookout with Karl. For a while now, Maura felt worse after seeing her friends than she did before she arrived. Everyone complained and they found less and less to laugh about. Even the name of the group, Moongirls, felt artificial, like a bad Halloween costume.

As everyone rose to get dessert and coffee, she backed away.

"I'm going now. I have to take a break from this. I love you all, you know that, but this is not working for me anymore and I don't know why. Sorry."

The women protested, stepping on each other's words like mewling kittens in a box. "What?"

"You've never missed a meeting before."

"It's only hormones!"

"No more green apple cake?"

"We need your apple cake."

"How will you know what's going on?"

Maura knew what she'd miss: rehashed divorces, dying parents, and the antics of distressed teenagers. Together, they'd endured miscarriages, mothering mistakes, and desert patches in their marriages. But Maura needed to spin away from all of it, the wheel of needs and responsibilities, free. Now, more than ever, she listened to her body, and her body wanted to move.

Driving home with the moon as her sole friend, she wondered about the land it illuminated and, as she parked, how the porch light exposed her shrivelling pansies.

Karl met her in the yard, waited while she watered the flowers, and walked with her across the dark pasture up the hill, the path they took together most nights, and where she'd been wandering every afternoon since their youngest started school. Her hand drifted away from Karl's into her pocket. He loved the land, this land that came from her parents, who loved him and died content knowing that Maura and Karl would care for it. Karl absorbed the movements of animals in the dark, the smell of the grasses, the direction of wind, and promise of rain.

"The land talks if you listen," he said.

So he'd noticed her restlessness, Maura thought.

His arm went around her shoulder. Her eyes lifted to the stars. She resolved to keep the moon in her eyeshot every evening, every early morning, too. It might have something to tell her. It kept waking her up at night like a spotlight on stage, but when it did, it left her calmer. The moon settled her down. She had no one to talk to about this, not even the Moongirls, and no language to explain it.

"The moon is watching me," she said to herself on the way back.

"She knows about change," was all Karl said.

As they approached the yard, Maura gazed at their old barn fitted with high church windows, her wedding present from Karl, her dance studio, her constant. She fitted her arm around his waist. As Karl opened the door, she bent to her pansies, perking up already, dark purple under the porchlight.

The day that stripped the trees naked, rain and wind drove Maura to the bookstore in the city. Maura leafed through pages of a book about the river Nile. Travel, was that what she craved? At random, she read: "Only two things in this world are innately good: water and one's mother." Maura shelved the book. All she needed was that one line. Whatever she yearned, it wouldn't ruin her as a mother. It would enhance, like water for pansies. It even validated her moon watching.

Maura asked for books about life transitions. The young man pulled titles from the Women's section.

"What about this one? *Taking Charge of Perimenopause.*"

Maura shook her head, smiling that this fellow, all of twenty, even knew what perimenopause was, but maybe everyone could see what she felt. A red velvet curtain rising in her.

Next, the bookstore guy offered *Men are Clams, Women are Crowbars.* Again Maura shook her head. Karl was the same, predictable as breakfast, lunch, and dinner and Friday night sex. No, this strange turbulence erupted, volcanic and furious, inside her. She had time now, and so much energy, but nowhere to put it, and it demanded all of her, but—

Thwack. Bookstore guy slapped a finale on the counter. *Skinny Bitch.*

"I gave this one to my ex-girlfriend, but she brought it back," the guy said.

Maura ran for the door and stopped short at the poster on it. The door blew open for a fresh-faced young woman, and Maura held it for her, took a picture of the poster with her phone, and hurried out.

She studied the photo in the van, windows open to the loud wind. Auditions for *Cats!* Maura had seen the original production of *Cats!* in New York on a student trip. Makeup and whiskers.

"I could be the ancient one," she breathed, to the storm wailing within her. She raised her window and breathed again, in gratitude to the wind, the moon, and her mother for guiding her here.

The lines of agile women and men in their twenties filled up the studio, testing her balance, her grace, at her first audition since she left her dance career to come home and marry Karl. The girls behind her, two of her former ballet students, whispered.

"From the back, she still has a dancer body."

"If you cut off her head."

Maura saw them in the mirror but bowed her head to the floor, feigning a neck stretch. Nothing has changed, she thought, not in twenty-five years. She exhaled and blew away the cattiness. She should have worn more makeup, to cover her lines, but then it would drip and distract her. Take me as I am, she thought, giving her face in profile now, neck tall. I've earned every mark. She showed the other side. And proud of it. Another long slow exhale. She moved her body, counting the reps. She stayed with her reps. It kept her steady, focused. The girls behind her hardly did any warm-up. They seemed to be watching hers, even following. Copycats, she thought. Watch me.

Maura depended on her warm-up, a routine she did every day, to keep her back straight, arms moving, legs high, stomach zipped up tight. Although there was nowhere else she'd rather be in that moment, her mind kept wandering. She tried to focus on her breathing, what she always told her students.

In this room full of insanely young dancers in the rows behind her, to transport herself into the zone of pure movement, she needed the music. If the tired, wrinkled pianist, glasses looped around her neck, shuffling through her binder, didn't start soon, Maura would lose her nerve. Flee to the washroom. Cry down the hallway. Slink back to the van.

The director, Raj, led the class. He'd had some dance training and was fit enough to practice most of the work with them. A standard ballet routine, a little jazz movement, no leaps or pointe work, a bit of basic choreography with turns, but it lasted ninety minutes. After the closing révérence, Maura dropped quivering spaghetti limbs to the floor and removed her sweaty old ballet slippers.

Raj, the replacement drama and music teacher at the high school, spoke. "Thank you, everyone." He seemed energized, inspired by their efforts. "I'd like the following dancers to stay, please…." Here he shuffled the pile of photos attached to résumés and called out a group of eight dancers: six women, including the two behind Maura, and two men. As the selected squealed to each other, the pianist, slowly, and the unselected, quickly, picked up bags and gear to leave. Raj crouched down to Maura and asked her to wait until he'd handed out rehearsal schedules and dismissed the chosen eight. Maura stood up and was introduced as dance captain.

When it was only the two of them, Raj held both of her hands.

"I'm so happy to have you in the show."

"Not more than I am," she laughed.

"You're a pro."

When he opened his arms to her, she hugged him anyway. "An old pro. I'm so glad I saw the poster."

She let go of Raj when the pianist tottered back in to fetch her glasses case, left on the keyboard at the highest notes, which she hit as she fumbled the case, startling them both.

Raj continued, "You know there's a role for you, but I also want you to be choreographer. That will give me more time to work on the singing." He took the opportunity to introduce Maura to the pianist, whose pursed face momentarily revealed beautiful teeth.

Raj asked Maura, "Do you live in town?"

"Forty minutes away. But I feel like I've come home." To myself, Maura thought, my older and wiser self. Their spontaneous hug was bonding, if unprofessional. Artistic attraction, she told herself. They remained in the studio another hour and tripped over each other's excitement, enthusing over the script, the schedule, the score, the cast and crew.

"We'll be working side by side for months. We'll read each other's minds," he said.

He didn't say *forever* but Maura filled it in for herself. She adored his Oxford accent. She'd found what would keep her sane, rebalance her. A new partner. An artistic partner. A sun to her moon.

Karl had never seen her on stage, never knew her as a dancer, "married her and buried her," as Raj said, on the farm. The kids protested that their friends would be weirded out by Maura in a cat suit, and Karl's coolness suggested that he feared his perfect life of prepared meals, organized household, available wife, and personal down time was at risk.

"Karl, this is only the beginning."

He listened, jaw set, when he didn't say what was on his mind. His horse face, Maura called it.

"I want to be involved in the annual musical every year and help Raj choose plays with plenty of dance numbers."

"But you'll be gone a lot. What if you get pregnant again?"

"No more kids, Karl. We decided."

"It made you happy before. Until this last time." He meant the one they lost, three years ago.

So he still hadn't given up hope for a son, Maura thought. "Karl, we're both on our way to fifty." The red velvet curtain was rising to the light of the moon and this time, the show, her show, would go on.

"It would keep us young," he pressed.

Hadn't he seen how that miscarriage aged her? She never wanted to put her body through that again. It had taken a full year to get her energy back, but now here she was, an erupting mess.

"I need to be feline." At his confused look, she said it again, "The show is *Cats!*"

"Feral." Karl looked at her as if he didn't know her at all. "You're all over the place. People have been asking why you're walking the country down. And then there's that guy you're working with. Nobody knows much about him."

"I need a little freedom," she said. "If you want me here at all."

"I thought the dance barn, the ballet lessons … isn't that enough?"

"Not anymore."

"Did I do something wrong?" he asked.

"It's me. And it's normal and natural. I want to dance, Karl. With other dancers."

Genuine surprise creased his face. Maura left it there. He needed time, she thought, to get used to it. His wife on stage, dancing, singing, acting, an entity entirely unknown to him. Working and creating with a male colleague whose intentions were entirely also unknown and therefore completely suspicious. And, Karl hated cats.

Maura scrambled to plan for the kids and Karl during rehearsal, six to nine, three nights a week, and all day Saturday. Because this was community theatre, rehearsals were scheduled around everyone's workdays. On the phone to Raj, she mentioned that her work on Mommy Island as mother of five and farmwife had been eighteen hours a day for over two decades.

"I'm going to put turkeys in the dance barn." Karl said.

"No way!" protested the girls.

"No," Maura said. "I need to plan the choreography, then practise it so I can teach the others. I'll be using it every day. If I didn't have the dance barn you made me, I'd never have this."

Karl was silent. Maura went out to look at the moon. She had so much to say and she would say it with movement, gesture, muscle. Fluidly, inspired by magical moon water.

Maura's oldest daughter reported, "The whole Grade Twelve drama class, including the one boy, is in love with Raj. He left England because he was *stalked* by an ex-girlfriend!"

That explained why Raj's experience made him ridiculously overqualified to teach high school and put on one community musical each spring. He was in hiding. Maura would need to be careful. People will talk, no matter what she did or what she felt or what she thought. Karl knew it, too.

"It's him," Karl growled. "It's dinnertime."

Maura took the call in the kitchen so everyone could hear and see as she marked in some new dates on the family calendar. Karl had walked, ridden, driven over the land, her land, their land now, for the years of her marriage while she remained plugged into the walls of her kitchen like the stove, the deep freeze, and the dishwasher. When she got off the phone, she cornered Karl.

"Raj will be phoning me a lot. He has the right to call me *anytime*. And we'll have meetings before and after every rehearsal."

"What about the kids?" It came out as *what about me?*

"Up to you," she said. Her dance captain voice surged from inside. "You'll be parent in charge."

He didn't give a comeback to that.

Maura agreed to prepare a crockpot meal on Tuesdays if Karl would provide a dad dinner on Thursdays.

"Dad dinners come in a flat box. And you can't criticize."

"They'll love it." Maybe, she thought, she'd never given him space in the kitchen before. It was time she let him in. And the girls. And herself out.

The kids would learn to cook on Friday nights and feed their friends themselves. The fridge would be full, as always. The dance barn would be open, as usual, to parties and sleepovers.

"But you have to be around to supervise," she said to Karl. "Not holed up in your workshop with your country music on full blast."

"On Saturdays," Karl said, "I'll pick you up after rehearsal, take you out to supper and the kids can eat their own leftovers." Friday nights would simply switch to Saturday nights. Flexible Karl.

But as Maura chopped onions for the soup, her thoughts

wandered to the umber skin of Raj. She wondered whether he was five or ten years younger than her. She inhaled the onions, letting go the tears that had simmered inside her all fall. She decided to wear the teaching skirt her mom had made many years ago to the first rehearsal. The skirt was deep purple, like her revived pansies.

She called Raj about costumes while she chopped celery and carrots and dumped them, leftover chicken, and stock into the pot. Maura knew a fabric artist who could paint everyone's bodysuits.

"I love that concept!" he said. "See you Tuesday."

Maura flipped the radio on. The kids were home, available for conversation, but she needed music after talking to Raj. He made her feel like dancing. His voice, his enthusiasm. She danced while she stirred the soup. Turns and leg lifts and, with spatula in hand, even a couple scissor-kicks.

"That's the first time I've seen you do that," said Susan, her middle child. "You only dance in the barn."

"I'm a cat on the prowl. I'm breaking out." She kept on. She was filling herself up, that gaping maw inside. She sang "Hello" with Adele. She was singing to Raj.

The girls pretended to be on their phones, but they were watching her. Probably texting emoticons to each other, making fun of her voice.

Maura read from behind Susan, "Our mom is turning into Catwoman!"

"It's important to her," Maura called out, like she would if one girl razzed another.

"Does that make us cat kids?" Susan said out loud.

Maura realized they'd been watching her their whole lives. She purred and pawed each of them affectionately, still dancing while the soup boiled over. This was the first time her girls hadn't changed the subject when she talked about the show.

"And Daddy's a wolf," Maura said playfully as she pulled the pot from the burner. The girls howled.

Raj was a Siamese.

A cat had more than one life. Each of her girls needed to see her grow. She needed to manoeuvre this better with Karl. The kids might assume that the marriage was over, like when one of her friends left her family and farm to be a barista in the city because "at least they pay me to wait on them."

Or when Maura's own mother painted a mural on the barn doors. Flowers, purple and yellow, danced around the border, but her father sloshed red over it the very next day, muttering that he'd be a laughingstock. Her mother took to making note cards with pressed dried flowers for craft sales. Maura remembered violets, Johnny-jump-ups.

When Karl came in a little earlier and toasted and buttered the bread while Maura ladled out the soup, she hugged him after he sat down. A kiss on his neck, in front of the girls.

"Meow," Susan said.

"Woof," said Karl.

Tuesday night, Maura parked in the gravel lot, dusted with the first snow, outside the theatre for the first rehearsal. She pulled out her clipboard, her dance bag, and a giant Tupperware of veggie snacks for everyone. She took a deep breath of snowy air. As she left the van, holding everything like a gift to the party, she performed a spontaneous little pas-de-chat, a private ritual she began the day of auditions. The studio lights were already on, the sky outside clear now, and hurrying to winter dark.

She would demonstrate how to lick the floor with the foot, stroke the air with the arm, and reach for the lights with her crown, all to the wildly liberating music of *Cats!* She craved some lifts in the choreography. She'd ask for separate sessions with the two men in the cast. If they could lift her! A goddess lift, her arms embracing the heights, in her own light.

She looked up at the sky, and yes, a single star peered out already. She'd need a mass of sequined stars for the drive home after ten tonight, to pin her back to the land and Karl, because Raj and the show could shoot her into orbit. The moon was half-full tonight, partially behind cloud. She hoped to see it later, to meditate on its greatness, steadiness, wisdom. Along with another pas-de-chat, a nightly ritual true to her cat self.

Raj met her inside the door, his hand already on her shoulder, setting off flares. "Maura. Ready to leap off Mommy Island?"

He had no idea how much. And what it could cost her if she touched the three-day growth on his chin.

"I want to dance till I'm dead."

She passed him the oversized Tupperware and kept her clipboard and dance bag in her own two hands because she had a show to do.

Winning Chance

Chance hauled himself into Jeff's truck, glanced in the back and raked his hand under coffee cups and garbage for his tool belt. He traded take-out from Tim's for rides with Jeff so Tina could have their van. He didn't usually leave his tool belt behind.

"Sure in a hurry last night," said Jeff, who loaded materials every morning so Chance could help Tina.

"Soccer."

"Fun."

"Dress 'em, feed 'em, and get 'em there on time." Three more hectic weeks of soccer left.

"At least you have a life. A wife." Jeff spiralled on rewind: his monasticism, working ten-hour days, then weekend side jobs with his brother-in-law, a wizard in home mods for disabled seniors.

Chance cut in, "Where to today?"

"Moneybend."

"Kitchen redo?"

"Cupboards, ten years old, won't shut."

"We guarantee that?"

"She's paying. French White."

"Custom?" Ten years ago, but Chance would never forget that Riverbend address. He didn't even check the job roster. "I should take a sick day. Guts are pounding, man."

"Heading to Tim's. Need more coffee anyway."

If Chance called in sick now, they'd get crap jobs for two weeks. This one, minor repairs, with two guys, would take an hour. A class job Chance didn't want.

But Jeff did. And he couldn't work it alone. Another company policy, ever since.

"Better?" Jeff said, carrying a supersized double-double and a sprinkled donut.

The truck smelled raunchy, but her tropical scent unearthed in his memory and took over.

"Coffee helps. Let's go." Keep your head, don't look at her.

"Maybe she's rich and single," said Jeff. "There's one in Moneybend, the guys said. A doctor, too. What's her name?"

"Dr. Sandra Bates, radiologist." Chance said it without looking down.

"No freaking way."

"Maybe she won't recognize me. Four kids later."

"Never mind Tina. Hell of a wife."

Chance wondered how Sandra picked him. Maybe she tangled with every tool belt. Cabinet makers come in last, so maybe she hadn't seen what she liked yet.

"Takes me out of the kitchen to see a problem with the bedroom window, she says. Locks the door."

"And takes off your tool belt," said Jeff, eyes wide.

"Went on for months. Then she got me tested. Said I had a low count."

"Hah."

"But I believed her."

"So that's what messed you up."

"Stay clear." Jeff's brother-in-law had pulled Chance back from the brink. But Chance knew that Jeff couldn't wait to drop his belt. The guys called him The Monk. Chance didn't, because he knew that pain. "Probably married by now. I mean, she has to have it every day."

Jeff was in Never-never Land.

"Keep your shirt on," Chance said to the sour air.

Tina, she'd see he had a hard day turn on kids' TV, and pull him into the bedroom. Before soccer season, anyway. Once, though, when the kids were magically scheduled on the same field, they raced them to their coaches, then moved the van near a ravine. Drove back to the games flushed and happy, with Timbits for everyone. The kids cheered because their uniforms said Timbits on the back. Tina promised to buy them again (score!) next time everyone had soccer at the same place. Chance had to get himself fixed. Four Timbits was their max. With Tina so hot and ready all the time, they decided on Freedom Four-T.

Dr. Bates answered the door.

"Call me Sandra," she said to Jeff in that hiss of hers.

Jeff said it with every opportunity. Chance stayed out of the way like the underling he was not. He checked for photos on the fridge. No wedding. No kids. No toys inside or out. He kept his eyes on his work, adjusting here, tightening there.

"Is that you?" Sandra's hunger distorted her ultra-smooth face.

"Yeah."

"Chance! The company said you'd left."

Jeff floated out to his truck at her sexy wave, which said maybe later, dude, if you can handle it.

Chance kept his hands going. It kept his voice steady, his

thoughts straight. When Tina had something to say, he'd draw her into the garage. It was usually about the kids, so better out of their earshot anyway. Clearing his work bench helped him organize what to say back. He listened without asking questions before trying to fix things. Tradesman's secret. He hoped it would work with Sandra, because with that streaked hair, the tanned face, the bright eyes, and perfect model mouth and teeth, she didn't look a speck older than before. Made him realize he appreciated a little age on a woman, a mature self-confidence, honest knowingness, especially in Tina, other moms. Sandra probably had facelifts.

"Those reports were wrong," she said.

"I figured."

"How?"

"Seven, six, five and five."

Sandra looked away. At Jeff outside, deep breathing, pulling himself to his full height, eyes taking in her property, her car, professional landscaping. When she came back to Chance, Sandra's eyes glossed.

"I tried to call you."

"Thought you made it up."

"I needed to know."

"Who to blame."

Sandra's shoulders trembled. "I have all this." She waved her arms around the house, the grounds overlooking the river, the fountain trickling, and her red Mercedes in front. "But nothing compared to you. Four? How many of each?"

He packed his tools into his belt. Those numbers were not for her.

"When you dumped me you stole years of my life I won't get back. So that's what you have. Your cabinets are fixed. Should last a lifetime."

He would never use French White, ever, in his kitchen, which really needed redoing, but Tina would rather invest in the kids' music lessons and couldn't be without a kitchen for even a day.

On his way out, Chance couldn't resist gazing down the hall to the salmon pink room where sleek Sandra had steamed him in her hot tub, hand-fed him fruits he could not name and, surrounded by woodsy candles and spiced flowers, he'd kept her oiled for sixty-three nights. He'd stewed about her for over seven hundred more, then took another three hundred and fifty to flush her out of his system.

Then he met Tina at Home Depot. He was picking up a screen door for his counsellor at AA who turned out to be Jeff's brother-in-law. For the guy's mother. A pity job. Borrowed his truck, even. But Chance still had his tool belt. Never pawned his tools. A part of his hands, in a pack on his back the whole time he was homeless. Used occasionally for self-defence. Tina rang up the screen door. He noticed her nails were natural, no paint. Chance, freshly shaved, gulped in the lumber smell, the energy of the hardware store at eight on a late spring morning, back in the land of the living and raring to do a job, any job, before calling his old boss to say he was clean.

Tina put down a Home Depot card with her cell number on it and said, "Waited three whole years to give this out. I have specific requirements. If you want to know, meet me at Tim's for coffee."

First day back working and already, trouble with a woman. He looked across at Tina, tall as him, orange work apron tied tight, and felt himself smile back without any effort at all. Time dropped away.

He heard her say, "Next?" She was about to snatch back her card.

His hand intercepted it and tucked it into his heart pocket.

After installing the screen door plumb as could be, eating goulash with the yakkity-yak customer, and getting paid in crisp cash, he called Tina. He showered and craved not only Tim's coffee with her, but steaming soup, toasted bagel, and a cinnamon doughnut.

They went over their schooling, families (both had no brothers or sisters), work, TV shows, and music groups. Her bare long lean arms promised long, lean legs under her jeans. She waited.

He asked, "Your … um … requirements?"

"Funnels down to this: no drinking."

Too quickly he said, "Been off it a whole year and don't miss it at all."

"That's all I want. What about you?"

Here Chance took his time. He had to say. Could be a game-changer. Best to roll that boulder out of the way right now. He fumbled with his soup spoon, stirred his cold black coffee. Tina stopped it, her hand on his.

"Chance, what?"

"I can't have kids."

"Can't or don't want?"

"Always wanted. Wish I could have given my folks grand-kids before they went. What about you?" He moved his hands to support both of hers while he waited. The silences between them felt like a privilege.

"I should have been adopted," Tina said. "Instead I had a mom who drank herself to death. So adoption works for me. And bonus, no birth control."

And then she took him home.

She was there now. The kids were all in school till lunch. If he called in sick now, he and Tina would have the late morning in their bedroom. He loved the way the light made it golden by ten-thirty in June. They hadn't had the morning in years. It would give them opportunity for preamble, which normally they never had time for, so did without. Maybe he'd massage her back, which bothered her since birthing the twins, boys eight pounds each. After, they'd have lunch with the kids at the picnic table. He'd share from his lunch cooler—they'd love that—then he'd walk the girls and the dog back to school. The boys would muck in the sandbox and he and Tina would leave off gardening and lawn mowing and laundry and cleaning to share the sun and a near beer and watch The Twin Network, they called it. He'd order pizza for dinner and drive the kids in the van to pick it up so Tina could have a half-hour to herself. They both knew what that meant for later.

Chance placed his tool belt on top of his cooler on the truck cab floor and said to Jeff, "Take me home." He knew Jeff would return to Sandra's right after. She'd put her spell on him.

"We both got food poisoning, hey, Chance?"

Snakebite, Chance thought. "Yeah. A fancy bakery in Riverbend, because do you see a Tim's here?" Chance got Jeff hired, a favour to Jeff's brother-in-law, so he should cover for him. But when Chance called in to their boss, he might say, "Today I need to be with my wife, my kids, at home. Never send me back there again." Should have said it before. Chance wondered why he never did. Probably, to forget. Or, to see what he would do.

"Home," he said again, in a whisper.

The Winter Police

I'd been storing rainwater for months. Mom's old rain barrel, half the height of the house, was full. Hops that refused to die covered it completely. Three trees shaded it. Only a little healthier than the others, those three would become conspicuous when all else yellowed. They survived because of my scant watering, but also because they were bunched together. Like Kent, Mitch, and me.

No ice for thirty years, no snow for twenty, we'd lived with the water rations for a decade. My rainwater contained too many toxins for human consumption, but the trees welcomed what I could spare.

The thin squeal of an electric golf cart alerted me.

"Get in, quick," I said, checking for eyes in the back alley as Kent trundled an antique refrigeration unit into my green-hut door.

"Anyone out there?" Mitch said from inside, taking one side of the box to help Kent.

"Only a magpie," I said. The last kind of city bird, sustained by an ability to eat anything.

"Hey sis, you got enough water?" asked Kent.

"Shh." I whispered at Kent. The threat of sound biters or photo prods existed everywhere, even in our residential lane. I closed the door. "Enough for ten solid centimetres."

"I did the math," Mitch said. "We siphoned a sample with old garden hose last night. A little green with algae buildup, but Sonia's bleach got rid of it."

I'd saved the bleach, now contraband, from Mom's things, along with our skates, woolen socks, shovels, and skis.

"I brought paint for the lines," Kent said. His wife Maggie painted. It helped keep her sane because she hardly left their apartment.

As a registered grower, I had a greenhut covering most of the yard and regular drop-offs of plant liquid (that's what they called grey water) for the crop, mostly marijuana, because it had the best value. People were less interested in eating than staying high. Without water or wind, all food production happened indoors: hydroponics like my greenhut and indoor animal sequestration yards. Outside, a few untended trees with deep roots survived each drier, warmer year ("warmer" was a euphemism). Air conditioning was outlawed, as was refrigeration, so everybody lined up for half-rotten food doled out at central "cold" stations. Food lost its nutritive value by the time we procured it. Getting high to feel hungry enough to eat was the new normal.

Mitch, Kent, and I had built my greenhut over Mom's outdoor swimming pool. Dry for years, of course, and illegal way before Mom got sick. Near the end, her only solace was floating in that pool, her red bathing cap on, her wiry body always tanned, one of us on the lookout. The pool, only filled to one metre, remained covered at all times, even with her in it. Especially with her in it.

We waited until the red and blue lines dried and then Kent turned on the refrigeration unit and flooded the pool floor.

The plan came to me when, at the bottom of Mom's skate bin, I found my double-bladed toddler skates and hugged them to my chest and sobbed. All through the rations, impositions, fines, and fault-finding, I hadn't cried. Those rusty little skates gave me the guts to build the rink for Kent's daughter and my niece, the only grandchild. Mom never met May.

We opened a trap door in the corner of the greenhut and descended a vertical swim ladder two metres to the pool floor. It had been a lane pool, so there was no deep end, perfect for a rink. No one, not even Kent's wife, knew. Only us three.

Mitch decided to video the process: loonie at centre ice, oldtime slogans painted on the walls (remember Mountain Dew, Molson Canadian, or Air Canada?), and one raggedy net we liberated from the dump by feeding pot cookies to already lethargic watchdogs. I repaired the net; Mom taught me to sew. Mitch uploaded his video on an obscure revolutionary platform, *Winter*. To us, winter meant falling snow. The flicker of flakes on our tongues. We loved the cool, fresh promise of snow. As children, we made tracks with our boots on fantastical sparkling crystals. We made paths with our shovels, creatures from snow boulders, and ice slides with our sleds. In winter, children could alter the landscape. We wanted to share that magic with May.

As kids, Kent and I and Mitch played hockey on Dad's backyard rink. Mitch hung out at our place in summer, too, because of the pool. Mom taught us all to swim, even though it was obvious to her that neither swimming nor skating had any future as recreational sports. For a time, the very elite were chosen for government hockey careers—not the exorbitant sums of the old national leagues, but a kind of circus job at low pay. People did it for the love of the game. I sure would have if they'd asked me. But now pools and rinks were completely outlawed. To swim now, people had to walk out many kilometres from the crumbling coastline to the stinking ocean (iceberg melt had long ago raised sea levels, which had dropped equally fast when worldwide precipitation dwindled). To avoid garbage and plastic islands, a full drysuit, oxygen tank, and sealed headgear were required. Only the very wealthy ever ventured out. Rivers were bare rocks. Lakes, cracked mud. The words for creek, pond, stream, waterfall, glacier, iceberg—hardly used—became silenced.

Because of Mitch's video posts, the ice room meme went viral within minutes and thousands of people requested guides on how to build one.

Mitch provided information without revealing our location.

But people found us anyway. The kind in uniform, enviro cops, checking this and that with vague non-orders.

"They've noticed the energy spike," I said. Electricity, exclusively solar powered, was strictly monitored. I wish we'd had the materials to set up our own off-grid energy, but solar panels were no longer being produced.

"Turn off your grow lights for a few hours a night. That will confuse them. Sun's freaking hot enough," Kent said.

But the same two guys, a rookie and one my age, came back. They sampled the weed. (Mitch, Kent, and I never did, but I kept a stash for when any of us faced the end; I'd bought it for Mom to relieve her pain, which generated the decision to grow it). The cops hung out for hours, watching me work, getting in the way.

To ignore them, I pictured May, her pale hair and skin, but strong limbs from an inside exercise gym created by Kent, a skylight, and the baby veggies I cultivated in pockets between the marijuana. The first time we took her down to the rink, how her eyes had twinkled! Her hands clapped the faded mittens knitted by Mom for Kent, lifting up scrapings from the shovel Kent used to smooth the surface of the ice. I so wanted to let her lick them, but gently redirected her handful of ice to her cheek instead to feel the coolness, the wet. The rising colour in her face, the same hue as the mittens. A mitten fell off and the crystals melted into droplets in her little hot hand. She pushed a chair across the length of the ice, then pulled off her kiddie skates and her socks and shoes and squealed at bare feet on ice before Kent scooped her up and pretended to nibble her chilly toes. I kept May's giggling in my ear now to keep me calm, fight fear.

In prison, there were no fans. They were legal in your home, as long as you kept under your kilowatt max. In prison, part of the punishment was roasting like a meat on a stick (totally illegal now, a carbon crime, but no wieners or processed food remained). The penal code had narrowed exclusively to environmental infractions. People could do whatever they liked to each other, and some did, but most were occupied by subsistence. There were no schools or hospitals anymore, but most folks helped each other because that was the only way to survive. Our refrigeration unit counted as an earth crime, bad as the retro chest freezers some oldsters kept plugged in during the heat of the day and climbed into at night for a few hours of cool rest. There was zero tolerance for the ultimate form of greed, staying cool from energy-sucking air conditioning or possessing carbon-emitting refrigeration. The penalty was prison, fed only from waste trucks and work without rest on the power stations until death.

"What's this?" One of the officers fingered Kent's red plaid jacket, once our Dad's, hanging from the hook on the wall, not properly hidden by my silicon apron. About twenty-two, the curious one kept a carefully trimmed beard. (Shaving was no longer permitted, along with baths, showers, diuretics including coffee, tea, and alcohol of all kinds. And children.)

"My brother's. A relic. He wants me to make a pillow out of it," I said. Reuse of any kind was not only promoted but essential because manufacturing, innovation, industry—all of it—halted.

The cop sniffed the jacket. "It's been worn recently." He handed it to his partner. This one, bald with a Santa beard, was old enough to recognize the smell of wet wool.

Kent had recently left after putting down another layer of rink water. The plaid sleeve must have come undone at the cuff and dipped in the hose.

"Yup." The old guy took another whiff and was gone, remembering. His eyes fluttered closed. His stern mouth relaxed into a grin.

"I'm sorry. I must have spilled," I sputtered.

But it was no use. The hoses gurgled, dripping plant liquid from a computerized tank. The system was ultra-efficient, designed not to waste a drop.

"Her juice," Mitch said. Fruit juice was legal, if you could find a bearing tree. Most people drank the hydration concentrate supplied by the government. No one knew what was in it, but a chemist on another website, *Black Hole*, had done a test and found six hundred substances, many unrecognized by her.

"What kind of juice?" the younger one asked, salivating.

"Apple," Mitch continued, showing the heritage tree we'd moved inside the greenhut to prevent it from scorching. The healthy specimen graced a huge pot that covered the trap door. Mitch pointed out seven apples, almost ripe.

"Want one?" I asked.

The young one wrote that down and ignored me, but the older one flinched, reaching his hand out involuntarily, tempted.

"What do you do about bees?" he said, feeling the apple, its weight, its gloss. Fondling it, but careful to leave it on the branch. Old enough to remember the magic of bees. I showed my pollinating brush. It used to be for makeup. That became an off-list manufacturing item rather late; women didn't want to let go of cosmetics, but I had, long before the change in my own body (a heartbreak after many miscarriages), never mind the parching of the world. The old guy moved uncomfortably close to me.

"She's got ketones." He was smelling my breath; everyone smelled of ketones because of universal dehydration. "Not apple juice." He was salivating.

"Let's look around some more," said his partner.

Mitch and I stood as far away from the apple tree as possible, trying not to cling to each other. I mourned those seven apples. They'd be stolen before we were strapped in the barred police van. They were meant for May.

The officers searched the floor. It was made of scrap wood. The younger one, on his hands and knees, felt for drips, which led him to the trap door, not entirely covered with the tree pot as I'd instructed Kent, over and over.

Oh no. Kent. I had mentioned my brother, and he had an illegal child, which is why his wife never went out and had never seen or heard of the ice room. If Kent was caught, he and Maggie would be shipped to hard labour. May, not a chosen child permitted to the wealthiest, healthiest, and smartest people alive, would be executed.

The officers reached the bottom of the ladder.

Mitch motioned to lock them down there.

I shook my head. We couldn't have another charge against us. And they had zapguns, which stunned through doors, walls; they had camera optics to call the street police unit in milliseconds even if they were killed.

So we went down the ladder, too, to feel the cold for the last time.

"Saw this on *Winter*," said the young guy, impressed.

"Me, too," the old guy said. Most of the world's population had access to Internet, but only thirty percent had water. "It's beautiful. You've done a remarkable thing."

"Too bad it's going to cost you. Never been on a case like this before—could be fatal."

Mitch and I had calculated our risk as twenty-five years each—more than we expected to live, so we had accepted it for the sake of our niece. But Kent was only forty-five, his wife thirty, May two.

Mitch said, "You want to shoot a few while you're here?" He pointed to the hockey sticks, taped and retaped, the puck, hockey gloves, the restrung net.

"Oh, yeah," said the old one.

"This could be like an interactive hyperexperience. VR isn't the same at all." The young guy swung for a slap shot, and it hit the boards.

"The sound. It's the same sound!" The older officer laughed. He threw off his police hat, as if he'd scored a goal, dropped his gloves, pumped the air with his fist.

Kent's skates fit one, and Mitch's fit the other, but both stumbled numerous times and had to hold on to us. They were both working so hard that they didn't cool down right away in the subzero air. Euphoria glazed their eyes; glee pitched their calls and echoes. The officers' exuberant, spread-eagle hilarity pitted the ice, and I made a mental note for Kent to repair it. Then I remembered our fate. When the winter police emerged from their skating party, Mitch and I would lose this tiny world. We'd lose each other.

The bald one leaned on his stick as if listening to the pre-game national anthem and studied the artifacts on the walls: snowshoes, ice auger, toboggan, figure skates. "You know, Jake," he said, "this is a living museum."

"People would pay to come here," said Mitch. "They'd come from long distances." Mitch still tried. I loved that he tried to save the underground rink.

The cops stood tall in the skates.

Especially Jake. He had gained enough balance to look us up on his phone. An NHL referee now, wide stance, checking facts via his screen. "They have 80,000 followers. This could be your retirement project, Buddy."

I said, "How did you find us?"

Without looking up from his phone, Jake said, "Your brother. Wet shirtsleeve."

I wished Kent was on Hell's Subway by now (a last-ditch effort to save families, connected by cyberthwarts and safety phishnets). Maybe he got a message to Maggie to run with May.

"We stungunned him," said Jake.

Buddy, with new energy of a person half his age, paused from lacing his boots. "So I protect us from the high-up heat, you two and your brother work on water, machinery, and

ice maintenance, and whiz kid here brings in the customers."
He pointed to Jake. They locked eyes like two men jumping
off a cliff.

Mitch clasped my hand. "People need this," he said.

A shiver, a really good one, went up my spine. This one
cooled me right to my scalp. I focussed on May's red mittens, strung together, hung around a framed photo of Wayne
Gretzky, Mom's favourite hockey player.

But the ice room was for everyone. I should have known
that from the beginning. I squeezed Mitch's hand with all
the passion I had for him and our worn world.

"Okay," I said. "Let's get Kent."

We didn't argue about the money. People threw it around
like dead leaves now. The winter police shook freezing hands
with us, then led the way back up the ladder.

Love, Janis

It was because of Love that I survived. I wouldn't have made it without her. It's going to be the same for you, you'll see. I don't know if you can hear me, but I sense that you feel me here. And I'm staying all night. Your first night here, the nuns say, someone has to keep vigil. I'm going to call you Gloria. I can see the beauty you are, even with your face all beat up and your body bruised. After they found me, knee-deep in cast-off clothes and junk food packages and dirty points poking out of the carpet, I would have been left for dead except that the nuns heard tiny heartbeats.

The nuns took over from there. First they told the world that I was gone and then they slowly resurrected me out of my overdose so I could give birth. When I started to talk again, they whispered back at me about mother Mary and Jesus and the blessings showered upon me. My body was a wreck, as you know. They fed it and babied it and healed it; they took turns holding my body tight for six months, forcing the last atom of toxins out of me. They called me Sleeping Beauty. As if, huh? I never was no beauty. Not like you.

But I had guts. Tough guts, to come back from the beyond to deliver, fully awake, without pharmaceutical help, two perfect baby girls. I named them Peace and Love. We lost Peace hours after she was born, but I got to hold her close and sing to her and she heard me, that itty bitty thing. Her three hours of life was a gift, a blessing. When we lost her, the nuns and I, we sang our voices raw. Well, my voice was already raw. Always was.

Love slept through all that. And when she woke up, the nuns taught me how to breastfeed her. They assured me there was nothing bad left in me to pass on. By now, I believed everything they said. For a long time, I thought I was in heaven. I was in awe. I was stupefied. I didn't really under-stand what was real until Love slept through the night. It took me weeks to get that I was alive, that my one baby was alive, and we had lives to live. Then I woke up and started to cry. The nuns got me singing if I felt like crying, and that helped. Music was my drug, they said. They said my voice had power. I ate, fed Love, I sang.

The nuns pray all the time, seriously. While they work, while they eat, while they walk. That's what they're doing now, in the chapel. Can you hear them? They're praying for you, for me, for all of us. I started singing their prayers, rock style. They loved it. They even have me sing at Mass now. On a seawind chilled night, they found me a guitar in a back alley trashcan, and they gave it to me, with a package of new strings. They are garbage-pickers, these women. Angels who pick up debris. They only take in the weakest, most pathetic pregnancies, girls so crazy spaced out that their babies are not expected to—but yours will, Gloria. I can feel her in there, listening to me. I began to help by singing to the girls and their babies. I'm going to sing to you, if you want, when you open your eyes or even if you don't. I give them hope, some of them, I think, maybe the younger ones. The ones who'd never heard my voice before. They call me Hope, anyway. I'm not a nun. I am Hope.

My voice has mellowed a bit, but not much. It's full of scars. So. The nuns never asked me to leave and I never asked to go. I knew if I went back to my old life, even with Love, I could not survive. I am permanently wasted on the inside, but I would never, ever, risk the life of Love. I needed her and the sanctified ground of the nuns under me. I learned how to be a gardener and bit by bit I took over the flowers first, then the vegetables and grains.

And Love, she was my flower-fairy child. I took good care of her, but also gave her lots of freedom—within our nunnery walls, that is. Whenever I felt like jumping those walls, I did my own brand of meditative hallucination. The nuns taught me. They do it with prayer, but I stare at my flowers for a while and my brain takes over. It remembers the rush. The imprint, the pathway, is still there. I can actually relive the whole freaking feeling of being high! Without the stuff. Well, I only use grass, now. I've got my own stash planted so the nuns won't find it. It's enough. Just enough to get me there. And I use it on the girls. To calm them. Medicinal purposes. Hope. I'll teach you. After your baby comes.

Now that Love's away, travelling, I've been a bit lost. Thank God for girls like you, Gloria; you're all my babies now. The nuns educated Love, then encouraged her to go out and see the world. Besides, there are no guys here. Love, naturally, wanted to find out about men. The only man here is, uh, God, and well, you know, we all have to share Him. I let Love go, but I didn't tell her about Janis. Sooner or later she's going to get messed up in all that crap: hey, I know that hellish voice, she's alive, she's my mother! She'll want to know. I hope it brings her back, but the world is an intoxicating place.

If Love comes back for me, I'll go with her if she asks. In a heartbeat. But she hasn't. If I go out there to look for her, I'll have to sell my story to survive. That would mean the end of Hope, for me.

Yet even with my natural organic highs, I miss the joy. I never counted on having that joy, and it just blew my mind, every single day she was growing up. I miss Love so much, I'm either singing or tripping all the time now. I sing for Peace, too. I think about her all the time. I'll never forget her as long as I live. That tiny kitten body, alive, and then asleep forever.

I was the one who was supposed to die.

M & M

When Maurice and I met, through friends at the curling rink, we were both past looking for someone special. We'd both had lovers, never a partner, but soon found home in each other's arms. Before we set out in the car later that winter, we walked in the river valley. We found lace in frosted trees, longing in strings of waxwings, and eloquence in cracking ice. At the top of the trail, perched on a manhole cover, the only space free of snow, Maurice and I pledged togetherness with a ring that dazzled in the winter sun.

Snug in my small red Mazda, humming down Highway 16 from Edmonton to Jasper Park Lodge, Maurice's hand strayed from the wheel and warmed mine. Our families understood that we wanted to be alone for our first Christmas together. And that for my birthday on December 22, I wanted only Maurice.

"The age we fall in love, Marissa, is the one we are together, forever."

In his eyes I would never turn thirty-nine. He was forty-one. Maurice wiggled my diamond ring.

I dug in my bag. "Want some M&M's?" Friends kept giving them to us as gifts.

"Let's save the M&M's for the tables, as favours for the guests."

We agreed that everyone would know about the engagement and the wedding, as soon and as simple as possible, when we returned. For now, the news would be savoured by us alone.

I patted the family-sized package of M&M's on my lap.

For his first gift of the season, I had packed Napoleon wineglasses in honour of his French heritage. I anticipated filling the glasses—Maurice hid champagne, but I spied it—and the chime as our glasses touched. I stashed eleven other presents, one for each of the twelve days of Christmas, but the wineglasses were for that night.

"Oh, no. Guess what I forgot."

"Me, too." We laughed because we brought gifts, not birth control.

More than anything, we wanted to put the icy road behind us and build a fire.

Maurice was driving and it was snowing, but at that moment we were looking at each other, agreeing to let the stars decide about a baby. So we didn't see what happened at all.

A trucker was heading toward us with a load of pipe for a gas service unit east of Edson. Mountain routes were his specialty. His truck, a black Mack, had eighteen wheels. Chester, a trucker for fifteen years, sustained minor injuries.

We became guardians, stationed above Highway 16. We were tethered to the earth by light, tangled in the stars.

In the year we'd been suspended above Highway 16, we searched for a way to be free.

In his counselling sessions, Chester said he saw us for a second—he woke up and veered off, hoping to glance off the left front headlight of the Mazda. Chester considered the angles again and again. The illumination wasn't from his high beams, because they had steered right. Yet at his left, he saw us, face and eyes joined in mysterious light, the moment before impact.

After months of classes and tests, Chester climbed back in his truck. One night at dusk he stopped at an alpine meadow and stretched out on his back in the autumn grass. Gradually the sky, like a mother, pulled over a comforter of stars. Chester, full of wonder, sank into the earth, muscles, fascia, skin, and bone. From that moment, he committed himself to stargazing. He collected books, an ultrasensitive telescope, and a new camera for night shots. He was looking for us.

We kept track of him, too. But we also looked for love in winter. It was all we knew. Because it had kept us together so far, we believed that winter love would release us to the big beyond for all eternity.

Maurice found her. For Maurice, life led to love.

"See the pink toque? Look at her *joie de vivre*."

A young woman, loaded with gear, hitchhiked on the resort road as late afternoon snow wafted down and a silver car crept out of the congested Marmot Basin parking lot. The driver, Wendy, a woman my earthly age, slowed to a stop.

We approved, and shone a little closer.

"We need gas in town anyway," Wendy said to her husband Grant.

That word, *husband*, embodied an ache we carried from earth. As did the other, *wife*. We had still not let go of them. Even now. Especially not now.

"And coffee," says Grant. "This could be tough going. I'll take the second shift."

"*Merci*," the hitchhiker trilled, dark hair spiralling out of her pom-pom toque as she loaded her snowboard into the trunk. "I'm Chantelle," she said to the boys in the back seat. "From Trois-Rivières."

Une belle Québécoise. That pleased Maurice even more. He whistled at the clouds, and they spilled lazy saucer-sized flakes down the curvy mountain road.

Wendy's boys marvelled at the weight of the snow. *It's puking*, they taught Chantelle, and giggled with her as they watched YouTube videos of funny dogs on the way to Jasper. After pumping and paying for gas, Grant shared around a big bag of M&M's.

"Oh," I said. "Look." The night we became guardians, peanut M&M's skittered and seeded the ice. Once the debris had been cleared, they remained frozen in, the only trace we'd been there at all. A great grey owl, hungry for the nuts embedded in the road, persevered a second too long. Knocked to the ditch by a truck carrying twin ATVs, her carcass, pulled by a lynx at first light, slid into the dark forest.

After being with the cozy family, Chantelle decided to walk the rest of the way to her basement suite rather than redirect the station wagon off its path. The car skidded slightly at the train station crosswalk. Wendy didn't notice, but I did.

"*Vous êtes des anges*," Chantelle smiled. "Angels in the snow!"

"Stay well," called Wendy, blowing back a kiss.

"*Vous aussi!* Mountain people are *ma famille*." But loneliness hooded her face as soon as she turned away. Her toque bobbed as she walked with her pack and board, but Chantelle missed her *maman au Québec*, "*tu me manque*."

Maurice noticed that behind Wendy, the truck driver gearing down to wait for Chantelle to cross the road was Chester.

Chester lined up his long rig against the curb and parked. Wendy's vehicle skidded again when she steered back into traffic.

"Maurice," I said, "we must move on. This may be our chance. Our task."

"Okay," he said. "*On y va*."

We followed Wendy.

The flurries blew from the northeast directly onto Wendy's windshield. The heavy German-built station wagon, loaded with skis, repelled the road, not sticking as it should. The tires hydroplaned as if swimming in summer rain. Wendy slowed down. Snow swirled and horns honked as truck drivers passed.

But not Chester. In his truck cab by the train station, waking after a much-needed nap, Chester prepared for the dark. Because Jasper National Park was a Dark Sky Preserve, Chester always spent the night there. He lumbered through the snow-dusted elk-bent grass with telescope and camera to dissipate the vision that haunted him nightly. Chester set up his tripod.

Maurice, distracted, looked back and stirred the Jasper sky clear for him. *Très gallant*, my Maurice.

I watched Wendy struggle on the Jasper Park road, and brought Maurice's attention back. Grant snoozed beside Wendy, oblivious.

"We could have been like them," I said. The work of years and children had trod a space between Wendy and Grant, but I could tell that alone, they were lovers.

"They could be like us," said Maurice.

The snow was hypnotic, limiting visibility, and Wendy strained to see the lights of the vehicles ahead. She dropped her speed again.

Then Wendy whispered, "I need you now."

I'd been called. I moved my light closer as the last vehicle behind her sped past.

The boys in the back seat wrestled. I blew in their ears. They settled down under jackets and blankets. This made Maurice beam. He had yearned for a little family, too.

Wendy pulled off the road. She peeled her palms off the steering wheel. Grant awoke to the sound of her gulping air, near panic. He held her hands until she regained her breath, then checked the tires, but nothing was wrong. Wendy got out and rotated her neck. She lifted her shoulders and dropped them suddenly to release the tension. She sucked in long breaths of cold air and slowed her breathing with long exhales. Grant walked her around the car, then took the driver's seat.

"She feels like he's saving her again," I said.

"That remains to be seen."

"Yes, but she believes it." Grant's hand had pulled Wendy back to him in dark seawater, in the labour room, on the ski hill. Wendy breathed deeply. Three hundred kilometres to go.

"It's worse where they're headed," Maurice said, looking beyond at the blizzard.

Maurice's gaze trailed back to Jasper. "I'll be with Chester."

"What? We vowed to stay together. We promised."

"He's calling me. Afraid of what he will see."

So I had to concede. Our joint light wrapped around our star, our two strands separated and projected down to our earthly work at different points on Highway 16.

It hurt to be apart from Maurice. I dropped crystal tears on the black ribbon of road ahead of Wendy and Grant.

My falling teardrops stippled the ice, and the tires stabilized. Grant drove the speed limit and sailed on for home.

Wendy gazed out to the stars, behind the snow. Although she couldn't see my light, it touched her face, and her neck finally relaxed. Since the snow had faded and the kids had conked out in the back seat, they didn't stop for more coffee or supper but kept driving through Hinton, Edson, Evansburg, and Entwistle to Edmonton. The path we took in reverse. They were almost home. At the lights of Stony Plain, on dry road, I left Wendy.

I joined Maurice back in the mountains as the moon crawled up behind the peaks. Chester focused his telescope to capture the moon in its perigee, but what he saw yet again was the look between us before my little red car burst into flames. We were a breath away from destruction.

Warmed by a bowl of *soupe à l'oignon gratinée*, her mother's recipe, and drawn outside by the moon, Chantelle approached the telescope on the grassy trail. She put her hand on Chester's shoulder and *s'il vous plait* asked if she could look, the instant before we exploded for the thousandth time. Chester moved away from the lens, and he heard bells in the pitch of Chantelle's voice. Not the screech of tires, crunch of metal, then awful silence.

"*Magnifique,*" Chantelle said to the bright winter moon, her round eyes looking up at Chester. Chantelle was younger than him, nomadic like him, and incredibly fit, which he was not. She was the first to witness his wonder at us, now fixed as a brilliant still shot of love in his brain. No horror movie, no collision, no fire.

Maurice sent a shooting star over the mountains, under the moon, as applause. Chantelle and Chester clasped hands in delight.

Gazing at the mountains reaching for the dark blue sky, Chantelle dreamed of a log cabin in the snow. The path of the falling *étoile filante* conjured a semi-circle of children with rusty hair like Chester, a big black dog, *de la soupe* simmering on the stove, a round of Brie, and a telescope in every window. Chester's vision matched Chantelle's, but included the trade of his long haul truck for an astronomy course and a Parks Canada uniform.

At the same instant, Wendy stroked Grant's hand and the station wagon slipped on a patch of black ice. Grant knew that on ice the only choice was to wait out the skid and keep the wheels straight. The exact moment that Chantelle looked back at Chester, the silver station wagon landed off kilter. Wendy cried out, startling the boys. I heard her thumping heart as if it were mine.

In that moment Chantelle's wide smile illuminated Chester's face, and his eyes, hers.

The light between them also severed the strands that attached us to earth and rocketed us, entwined, to the highest heavens, way past the Milky Way, the round Brie moon, unspoken words, face and eyes, snowflakes on lynx fur, multi-coloured M&M's. We cast our hope into the abyss below, to the outskirts of the city on Highway 16, in the bouncing station wagon where Wendy and Grant looked at each other.

Acknowledgements

These stories were developed with the gracious help of my first readers, Margaret Macpherson and Laurel Sproule. The Writers Guild of Alberta Mentorship Program introduced me to Myrl Coulter, a wonderful new writing friend who worked with me on a handful of these stories and encouraged me in the art of short fiction from beginning to end.

"The Exchange" first appeared in *Epiphany* (Fall/Winter 2016); "The Care & Feeding of Small Birds" was printed in chapbook form by Loft 112 in Calgary in June 2017; "Sunset Travel for Single Seniors" was published in *Room* 40.3 (Fall 2017); "M & M" was featured in *Grain* 44.2 (Winter 2017); and "Belovèd by the Moon" was included in *The Prairie Journal* 70 (Fall 2018).

Many thanks to the Alberta Foundation for the Arts for a marketing grant for this collection.